Night and Day

Also by Tom Stoppard

ROSENCRANTZ AND GUILDENSTERN ARE DEAD

THE REAL INSPECTOR HOUND

ENTER A FREE MAN

ALBERT'S BRIDGE

IF YOU'RE GLAD I'LL BE FRANK

AFTER MAGRITTE

JUMPERS

ARTIST DESCENDING A STAIRCASE

and WHERE ARE THEY NOW?

TRAVESTIES

DIRTY LINEN *and* NEW-FOUND-LAND

EVERY GOOD BOY DESERVES FAVOUR

and PROFESSIONAL FOUL

and a novel

LORD MALQUIST AND MR MOON

Night and Day

TOM STOPPARD

FABER AND FABER

LONDON   BOSTON

First published in 1978
Second edition published in 1979
by Faber and Faber Limited
3 Queen Square London WC1N 3AU
Printed in Great Britain by
Latimer Trend & Company Ltd Plymouth
All rights reserved

All rights whatsoever in this play are strictly
reserved and professional applications to perform
it, etc., must be made in advance, before rehearsals
begin, to Fraser and Dunlop (Scripts) Limited of
91 Regent Street, London W1, and amateur
applications for permission to perform it, etc.,
must be made in advance, before rehearsals begin,
to Samuel French Limited of 26 Southampton
Row, London WC2

British Library Cataloguing in Publication Data

Stoppard, Tom
Night and day.
822'.9'14   PR6069.T6N/

ISBN 0–571–11372–9
ISBN 0–571–11373–7 Pbk

Author's Note

As in the case of some of my previous plays the first published
edition of *Night and Day* was the script as it had been offered
to the director, the designer and the actors, while this second
edition has been brought into line with the text which was
ultimately performed. Once again I have been the beneficiary
of the collective efforts of those involved and, particularly, of
the perceptions of Peter Wood who directed the play: to
them my thanks. I am also grateful for the indulgence shown
to me by the publishers.

T.S.

To Paul Johnson

Characters

GEORGE GUTHRIE
RUTH CARSON
ALASTAIR CARSON
DICK WAGNER
JACOB MILNE
GEOFFREY CARSON
PRESIDENT MAGEEBA
FRANCIS

Night and Day was first presented in London by Michael Codron at the Phoenix Theatre on 8th November 1978 when the cast was as follows:

GEORGE GUTHRIE	William Marlowe
FRANCIS	George Harris
RUTH CARSON	Diana Rigg
ALASTAIR CARSON	Jon Bentley/
	Andrew Parris
DICK WAGNER	John Thaw
JACOB MILNE	Peter Machin
GEOFFREY CARSON	David Langton
PRESIDENT MAGEEBA	Olu Jacobs

The play was directed by Peter Wood and designed by Carl Toms with lighting by Robert Bryan.

Notes on Characters

GUTHRIE is in his forties; perhaps quite short; fit, can look after himself; wears tough clothes, blue denim, comfortable boots.

RUTH is in her late thirties; probably tall; attractive in face, figure and, especially, voice; shoulder-length hair.

ALASTAIR is eight, English prep school; fair.

WAGNER is in his forties, a suit-and-tie man; big but not fat. An Australian; some accent.

MILNE is twenty-two or twenty-three and definitely attractive in a way that is called boyish; casually dressed.

CARSON, RUTH's husband, is somewhat older than she but also in good shape; casually but well dressed.

MAGEEBA, the President, is around fifty, a British-educated black African, a hard man if soft of voice; carefully dressed in freshly-laundered 'informal' army uniform.

FRANCIS, CARSON's black African servant and driver, is in his twenties; slacks and white clean short-sleeved shirt.

A note on 'RUTH'

The audience is occasionally made privy to RUTH's thoughts,
and to hers alone. When RUTH's thoughts are audible
she is simply called 'RUTH' in quotes, and treated as a
separate character. Thus, RUTH can be interrupted by 'RUTH'.
This rule is also loosely applied to the first scene of Act Two,
where the situation is somewhat different.

The Set

An empty stage with a cyclorama, representing the open air, and a living room share the stage in various proportions, including total occupancy by the one or the other. Thus, the living room is mobile. The first act begins in emptiness, continues in the interior of the Carson house and ends in the Carson garden. There may be intermediate positions for 'the room', leaving some space for garden. In the second act the stage is wholly occupied by the interior of the house. The important limiting factor is that the interior incorporates a study containing a telex machine which must be visible to the audience at different moments during the interior passages. The first scene, after the prologue, has been written with a view to there being a verandah area bordering the room on the garden side.

We are in a fictitious African country, formerly a British Colony. The living room is part of a large and expensive house. The furniture is European with local colour. It looks comfortable and well used. Essentials include two telephones, marble-topped table or sideboard with bottles and glasses on it, and a large sofa. The verandah also has suitable furniture on it, including a small table and a couple of chairs at the down-stage end. The garden will contain at least one long comfortable cane chair. The room should seat five people comfortably. It could be connected with the rest of the house through a door, more likely double-doors, or it might continue out of sight into the wings. The front door of the house might well be visible.

The first act—after the prologue—starts just before sunset, the last rays illuminating the garden; twilight follows quickly on this, and darkness has overtaken the play by the time of RUTH's second entrance.

Act One

African sunset.
An open, empty stage, the frame perhaps broken by the branch of a
tree. There may be a low skyline but not necessarily. The 'cyc' looks
very beautiful. The sun is nearly down. The sky goes through rapid
changes towards darkness.
A distant helicopter is heard approaching. By the time it reaches
'overhead', darkness has fallen and there is moonlight.
Helicopter very loud. Shadow of blades whirling on the floor of the
stage. Violent shaking of foliage. A spotlight from the helicopter
traverses the stage. It disappears. A jeep drives on to the stage with
its headlights on. Not much can be seen in the darkness. Two or
three people in the jeep. GUTHRIE *is one of the passengers. The jeep*
turns into the audience so one can only see headlights.
By the time the jeep appears, a machine-gun has started up. The
noise is all very loud—helicopter and machine-gun. The jeep
*probably isn't audible. Someone—*GUTHRIE*—shouts something about*
the lights, and the jeep's headlights are turned off. The jeep hasn't
stopped moving. It is turning in a circle. The spotlight comes back
and sweeps across the jeep. GUTHRIE *jumps out of the jeep and runs.*
He doesn't leave the stage. He just runs out of the light. The light
loses the jeep. The jeep goes. GUTHRIE *crouches in a down-stage*
corner. He is shouting but it is hard to catch. He is shouting 'Press!
Press! You stupid fuckers!' Then the spotlight finds him. He stands
up into the light with his arms spread out, shouting. The gun is
firing bursts. He moves away from the corner. A burst catches him
and knocks him over.

A late afternoon light reveals GUTHRIE *stretched out on a long garden chair. Sundown. The steps to the verandah and the room are behind him. The telex is visible and chattering in bursts like the machine-gun; it is apparent that the noise of the telex had entered* GUTHRIE's *dream in the form of machine-gun fire. The noise has continued right through the transition of the scene. African 'rock' music is playing on a cassette-player standing on the verandah. This sound is joined by the sound of an approaching car. The telex stops. Not far from* GUTHRIE's *chair is his camera-bag, with pockets for cameras, lenses, exposed and unexposed film, and other small objects. An empty glass is lying near the chair.*

GUTHRIE *is apparently asleep.* FRANCIS *enters and removes the empty glass and goes again. The car arrives. The car door slams.*

RUTH *enters carrying two or three packages which she puts down.*

RUTH: Oh, those drums, those damned drums.
  (*She switches off the cassette-player. Then she sees* GUTHRIE *on the chair in the garden.* FRANCIS *enters, arranging table and chair, etc., for tea.*)
  Francis, there's a man under that tree.
FRANCIS: Yes, ma'am.
  (*He goes out.* RUTH *comes down and looks at* GUTHRIE, *who doesn't move. She notices the bag and bends down and touches it, perhaps to peer inside it.*)
GUTHRIE: Please don't touch that.
RUTH: I'm sorry.
GUTHRIE: Christ. That wasn't nice at all.
RUTH: I thought you were asleep.
GUTHRIE: I thought I was dead.
  (*He has barely moved and now doesn't move at all.* RUTH *looks at him.* FRANCIS *re-enters with a tea-tray.*)
RUTH: Thank you, Francis. Has the house been opened to the public?
FRANCIS: What's that, Mrs Carson?
  (*This gets through to* GUTHRIE.)
GUTHRIE: Oh—God—I'm terribly sorry—

RUTH: I shouldn't get up; you look awful. (*To* FRANCIS *who is leaving.*) Another cup.

(RUTH's *manner is easy-going.* GUTHRIE *gets up.*)

GUTHRIE: No—I'm fine. Sleeping on planes—you know. Ruins the complexion. From the inside. My name's Guthrie— George Guthrie.

RUTH: How do you do? I'm Ruth Carson. Would you care for some tea?

GUTHRIE: Wouldn't say no. Thanks.

(RUTH *is pouring tea for* GUTHRIE *into the only cup.*)

RUTH: Do you take sugar?

GUTHRIE: No thanks.

(*Meanwhile* FRANCIS *comes in with another cup.*)

RUTH: (*To* FRANCIS) Thank you. Would you take those parcels, Francis?

(GUTHRIE *is looking for something—saccharin tablets—in his bag.* FRANCIS *leaves with the packages.*)

I'm sorry I wasn't here to greet you Mr . . . Guthrie. I had to go into Jeddu to pick up some things.

GUTHRIE: The boy said it was okay to wait in the garden. Is that all right?

RUTH: Of course. But I'm afraid I have no idea what time Geoffrey will be home. He's been in Malakuangazi—I was expecting him this afternoon.

GUTHRIE: I've come to meet Dick Wagner. (*The name has the English form—Wag-ner. He has found the saccharin and is coming back to the table.* RUTH *remains perfectly still.* GUTHRIE *comes casually back to the table and sits down.* RUTH *waits until he looks at her.*)

RUTH: What are you talking about, Mr Guthrie?

GUTHRIE: Dick Wagner. Do you know him?

(*Pause*)

RUTH: Is he a composer?

GUTHRIE: No. He's a reporter. Writes for the *Sunday Globe*, in London. I take the pictures. The pictures, as you know, are worth a thousand words. In the case of Wagner, two thousand. He was supposed to be at KC to meet me.

RUTH: Why in God's name do you expect to meet him at my house?

GUTHRIE: He told me. He left a message at the airport.

RUTH: He told you to meet him *at my house*?

(GUTHRIE, *sipping tea, catches her tone for the first time, and hesitates.*)

GUTHRIE: Well, he didn't mention *you*.

'RUTH': Help.

GUTHRIE: Just the house. The boy said to sit in the garden till Wagner comes. Is that all right?

'RUTH': Is that all right? Oh yes—bloody marvellous. Just what you needed, Ruth, and serve you right. Nothing is for free, you always pay, and Guthrie has brought the bill. Silly woman!

GUTHRIE: Mrs Carson?

'RUTH': Oh God, get me out of this before Guthrie's friend arrives. I don't feel up to being witty today.

GUTHRIE: Penny for your thoughts?

RUTH: Sorry?

GUTHRIE: You were miles away.

RUTH: Alas, no.

GUTHRIE: Sorry?

(*Pause*)

RUTH: What kind of camera do you use?

GUTHRIE: Do you know anything about cameras?

RUTH: No. (*Pause*) By the way, we don't call them boy any more. The idea is, if we don't call them boy they won't chop us with their machetes. (*Brief smile.*) Small point.

(GUTHRIE *holds his arm out, palm to the ground.*)

GUTHRIE: Boy about this high, fair hair, your mouth, knows about cameras, has a Kodak himself; said I could wait in the garden.

(RUTH *acknowledges her mistake, but* GUTHRIE *pushes it.*)

His name's Alastair.

(*He has pushed it too far and she snaps at him.*)

18

RUTH: I know his bloody name.

GUTHRIE: (*Olive branch*) The one I use mainly is a motorized F2 Nikon. (*Sips tea.*) Lovely.

RUTH: (*Smiles*) Would you like a proper drink?

GUTHRIE: (*Relaxes; shakes his head*) The sambo gave me a lime squash. (*Winces*) Sorry. (*His hand chops the air twice.*) Chop-chop.

(RUTH *gets up; moves.*)

RUTH: Why is my husband filling my house with journalists?

GUTHRIE: I thought he was one.

RUTH: Geoffrey? Don't be silly.

GUTHRIE: I saw the telex.

RUTH: That's for his business. Did he ask this man to come here?

GUTHRIE: I don't know.

RUTH: What does he want?

GUTHRIE: I don't know.

'RUTH': Help! (*Piano chord.*)

GUTHRIE: A story maybe.

'RUTH': I need somebody—help—

(*Piano chord: it's the Beatles' song, 'Help!'.*)

GUTHRIE: What is his business?

'RUTH': (*Picking up the rhythm*) Not just anybody—He-e-e-lp!

(*Car approaching.*)

GUTHRIE: Somebody coming.

(GUTHRIE *stands up and moves back into the garden looking out. Piano cuts out.* RUTH *laughs briefly at herself.*)

GUTHRIE: (*Reporting from the garden*) Beat-up Mercedes. Is that your husband?

RUTH: It's a taxi.

GUTHRIE: (*Looking out*) Wagner.

(RUTH *leaves. She goes into the house.*
Helicopter approaching fast and low. GUTHRIE, *in the garden, looks up surprised. He sees the helicopter apparently coming straight at him. He cowers and goes into a crouch, his hands over his head. Shadow whips across the garden. Then the*

19

helicopter has gone.

The room now occupies the stage. GUTHRIE *is crouching over his bag, taking a pill-bottle from it, removing a pill, swallowing the pill.*

ALASTAIR *has entered. He sees* GUTHRIE *crouched.*)

ALASTAIR: What's the matter? Mr Guthrie?

GUTHRIE: Hello.

(ALASTAIR *is carrying an old-fashioned leather-bound Kodak. The camera is folded and* ALASTAIR *holds it by the strap.* GUTHRIE *straightens up.*)

Hello.

ALASTAIR: I've found it. Are you going to show me about it?

(*The receding helicopter noise has been succeeded by the taxi stopping outside the house. A dog barks, but not for long. Taxi departing.*)

GUTHRIE: I think my friend has arrived.

(FRANCIS *enters, not from the front door, carrying the cassette-player, which is playing again.*)

FRANCIS: Are you coming down to the compound, Allie?

ALASTAIR: No—I want to talk to Mr Guthrie.

(FRANCIS *leaves.*)

I came before but you were asleep.

GUTHRIE: I'm sorry.

ALASTAIR: Will you show me later?

GUTHRIE: Sure.

ALASTAIR: I believe this is an excellent camera. It just needs some film.

GUTHRIE: When does your daddy get home usually?

ALASTAIR: That was him. The helicopter.

GUTHRIE: Oh.

(*Another car drives away from the house.*)

ALASTAIR: He buzzes us. Then Francis takes the car down to the compound to fetch him.

GUTHRIE: The compound?

ALASTAIR: The mine. It's not daddy's own helicopter. He's just allowed to use it. A helicopter is extremely useful in a country like Africa. Have you ever flown in one?

GUTHRIE: Yes, a few times.

ALASTAIR: In Africa?

GUTHRIE: No, in Asia.

ALASTAIR: Well, you know how useful they can be.

GUTHRIE: Yes. This is my friend, Dick Wagner.

(WAGNER *has entered.*)

WAGNER: (*Enthusiastically*) Hello Gigi, you lovely bastard! (*He moves down into the room and slaps* GUTHRIE'*s shoulder.*) You look *terrific*!

GUTHRIE: I look terrible.

WAGNER: (*Fresh start; same tone*) You look *terrible*! How are you?

GUTHRIE: This is Alastair Carson.

WAGNER: (*Talking down*) How do you do, Alastair? And how old are you?

ALASTAIR: Eight. How old are you?

WAGNER: Kid's a natural.

(*Female voice off, not* RUTH, '*Allie!*'.)

ALASTAIR: Got to have my bath now, anyway. (*To* GUTHRIE.) Would you like to look at my camera 'til I get back?

GUTHRIE: Sure.

ALASTAIR: You won't forget?

GUTHRIE: No.

ALASTAIR: I'll come back.

(ALASTAIR *goes.*)

GUTHRIE: How are things here, Dick?

WAGNER: Not wonderful. I've been in Jeddu ten days. Bloody thing won't catch fire. Where's this Carson?

GUTHRIE: He's on his way. Who is he?

WAGNER: He runs the business end of the copper industry. Also manganese, potash . . . he's in mines generally.

GUTHRIE: But not frequently.

WAGNER: How about Mrs Carson?

GUTHRIE: She keeps herself nice, too.

WAGNER: Where is she?

GUTHRIE: Inside somewhere. Are you a friend of the family?

WAGNER: Hardly. The one who came out here was an earl or something. Grandfather, I think. There's an elder brother defending the title in England. This one works for a living. As it were. She's his second wife.

GUTHRIE: What are we doing here?

WAGNER: Looking up Carson.

GUTHRIE: Why?

WAGNER: I don't know. I think Hammaker must know him. (*He takes a folded cablegram out of his pocket.*) I got this on Sunday. 'Guthrie arriving KC ex-Dacca Thursday. ETA ten hundred. Suggest uplook Geoffrey Carson at home Jeddu. Happy birthday. Hammaker.'
(GUTHRIE *takes the cable out of his hand.*)
Did you tell her you were meeting me here?

GUTHRIE: Who? Oh . . . yeah.

WAGNER: You said me?

GUTHRIE: Yeah.

WAGNER: Dick Wagner?

GUTHRIE: How many names have you got?

WAGNER: How did she react?

GUTHRIE: A bit like you.

WAGNER: How's Dacca?

GUTHRIE: You know Dacca. It's not Paris.

WAGNER: (*Nods; sings badly*) 'April in Dacca . . . I love Dacca in the springtime. I love Dacca in the . . .' Yeah. It's not Paris. It's Dacca.

GUTHRIE: (*Handing back the cable*) Is it your birthday?

WAGNER: No. Sounds good, doesn't it?

GUTHRIE: Did you clock the telex?
(WAGNER *looks round and sees the telex.*)

WAGNER: Christ!

GUTHRIE: (*Nods*) Happy birthday.

WAGNER: I don't believe it.

GUTHRIE: Do you think he's got a wire machine somewhere?

WAGNER: We're going to make them sick.

GUTHRIE: Who's out here?

WAGNER: Everybody. (WAGNER *has gone to the machine. He taps a couple of keys and waits for the evidence that it is in working order. The machine chatters back at him briefly.* WAGNER *looks at* GUTHRIE *wide-eyed.*) We are going to make them *ill*.

GUTHRIE: The hotel doesn't have telex?

WAGNER: The hotel doesn't have cleft sticks. There's a post office in town which is a joke. Fritz Biedermeier said when he blew the dust off the counter there was an urgent message for Stanley from the *New York Herald*.

GUTHRIE: That wasn't here, was it?

WAGNER: It was a joke.

GUTHRIE: Okay. Who's Biedermeier?

WAGNER: *Newsweek*. He was in Beirut that time.

GUTHRIE: Oh yeah. Him. Has he got a photographer?

WAGNER: No, he's got a camera.

GUTHRIE: That's bad for trade.

WAGNER: Yeah, I wouldn't like it if you learned to write. I think we'll do okay. Especially now we've got wheels. Which is yours?

GUTHRIE: The Cortina.

WAGNER: Good. The taxi drivers have started to hire themselves out by auction.

GUTHRIE: How did you get up from Kamba City, then?

WAGNER: In a Cessna.

GUTHRIE: Bloody firemen.

WAGNER: Afraid of missing the war. It wasn't so expensive—I shared with a couple of photographers.

GUTHRIE: (*Interested*) Yeah?—who's that?

WAGNER: One was a Frog—Jean-Paul something. St Laurent army fatigues and a gold chain, very tough with the Gauloises, no filters—know what I mean? 'I was a Left Bank layabout 'til I discovered photo-journalism.'

GUTHRIE: (*Sharply, angrily*) Knock it off will you, Dick? (*Pause; apologetically.*) He's really very good.

WAGNER: Sorry.

GUTHRIE: What about the other one?

23

WAGNER: A groupie. No sweat. He had one of those cameras with a little picture of a cloud and a little picture of the sun and you slide it across according to the weather.

GUTHRIE: (*Smiles*) Well, I'm shooting Tri-X through two thousand quid's worth of lenses, but he'll get better pictures if he's in a better place. One time in Hué I was in a dug-out with Larry Barnes, and this American kid is there—he looked like a hippie, bummed his way into the country and got himself a letter from AP and a second-hand Leica, so he's accredited, right?—wouldn't know his arse from a hole in the ground except he's *in* a hole in the ground, and he's lost his light meter. He's reading his Kodak packet, and there's all kinds of shit coming over, mortars, and he says to Larry, 'Hey, do you think this is cloudy-bright or semi-dull?' Well, all you can see is smoke and flames, so Larry says, 'I think it's cloudy-bright.' This kid then starts walking forward behind a tank and the next time I see him he's got a set of prints of VC attacking the bridge, it looked like Robert Mitchum was just out of frame. Three pages in *Match*.

WAGNER: Maybe it's the same kid.

GUTHRIE: Later he stepped on a land-mine.

WAGNER: (*Pause*) It probably isn't, then.

GUTHRIE: And Larry. And the other three in Larry's helicopter. Do you know how many people were killed in that war?

WAGNER: Not exactly.

GUTHRIE: Forty-five.

WAGNER: Oh. People.

GUTHRIE: And eighteen missing.

WAGNER: Don't be morbid, Gigi.

GUTHRIE: I'm not being morbid. (*Pause*) Before you came I was sleeping, just over there, and I dreamed that I bought it—got killed by a helicopter. I was really quite spooked.

WAGNER: You were dreaming about Larry.

GUTHRIE: No—not in a helicopter *crash*—we were in a jeep, and this gunship was shooting at us. And then it killed me.

WAGNER: For Christ's sake!

24

GUTHRIE: Okay. How are they getting their stuff out?

WAGNER: Air freight from KC. There's nothing closer for pictures. Good chance of a pigeon, too—lots of people flying out at the moment. There's an overnight plane to London on Fridays—very handy; that gives you about twenty-four hours if you've got something for this week. And there's the AP wire on Saturday if you're pushed—they'll print up for you.

GUTHRIE: Yeh. I checked them out on the way up. Either way, it's a four-hour drive for that lot.

WAGNER: You won't do any better.

GUTHRIE: Carson's got a helicopter.

(*He sits down and picks up* ALASTAIR's *camera and opens it. He's going to find a roll of film in his own bag and put it into* ALASTAIR's *camera. But this is something which he takes his time over, checking the camera itself, etc. Also, he gets interrupted so the job isn't completed until later.*)

WAGNER: I can't take much more of this. Our own telex and a helicopter, and the competition writing postcards. If this war starts on a Saturday morning you and I are going to be famous.

GUTHRIE: You're famous in Dacca. I saw your name in the lavatory in the Inter-Continental.

WAGNER: How nice.

GUTHRIE: It said, 'Dick Wagner before he dicks you'.

WAGNER: (*Grins*) Sour grapes. That was a legitimate beat. I had my own source. By the time that Paki press officer handed it out with an embargo my story was in London—Jesus, it was on the *stone*.

GUTHRIE: All right.

WAGNER: (*Getting worked-up*) I mean, I *cracked* that story, Gigi. The embargo was just shutting the stable door—

GUTHRIE: Listen, it's nothing to me.

WAGNER: Yeh, but I know how those stuck-up bastards tell it around—the whole thing gets misreported.

GUTHRIE: (*Mildly*) And they're usually so accurate. Did you get

25

me a room?

WAGNER: You're with me. There's two hotels, both dumps.
Journalists hanging out the windows, and a Swedish TV
crew sleeping in the lobby, and a lot of good friends from
home too. We're going to make them ill. All we need is a
story.

GUTHRIE: Do you think we're in the right place?

WAGNER: What do you mean?

GUTHRIE: I don't know what I mean.

WAGNER: Well, everybody else is here.

GUTHRIE: That's what I mean.

WAGNER: There's nothing better. Except an interview with the
President, and nobody has even *seen* that mad bastard for
six months. Everybody's had a go.

GUTHRIE: What's the story in Jeddu?

WAGNER: (*Shrugs*) It's as near as we can get to Alf.

GUTHRIE: Who's he?

WAGNER: Them. 'Who's he?' Don't you ever look at the bits
between the photographs? Adoma Liberation Front. The
Colonel. Colonel Shimbu.

GUTHRIE: Okay.

WAGNER: Didn't you know about my famous scoop?

GUTHRIE: No.

WAGNER: Nor did I. Sunday, everyone gets cables. 'Globe finds
Colonel Shimbu. Why Colonel unfound by you', etcetera.
So everybody's screaming, where is he, Wagner, you
bastard? Only, it isn't my story. *I* don't know where the
bloody Colonel is. So they want to see my cable—they
think it's a herogram from Hammaker. But of course I can't
show it to them because I don't know what this happy
birthday thing is all about. So then they're calling me a
lying bastard, and following me to the lavatory when they
aren't following armoured car patrols into the bush in
broken-down taxis. You never saw anything like it.

GUTHRIE: Yes I did.

WAGNER: Yes you did. There's a government press officer here who's the usual lying jerk, but there's no way of telling whether he's lying because he knows the truth or because he doesn't know anything, so you can't trust his mendacity either—he could be telling the truth half the time, by accident. His line was that the Adoma Liberation Front didn't exist, and the army had got it completely surrounded. But the *Sunday Globe* knocked that one on the head. We heard it on the radio, the BBC World Service picked it up. And what do you know, George?—some sodding little stringer with no name has found Colonel Shimbu and made a monkey out of me. Yeah. It sounded like a good piece, too. I'd like to know how he got the story out. Interview with the Colonel himself, a party political broadcast wouldn't have done it better, and furthermore it's not a rebellion, it's a secession—get the picture? *Media credibility!* Well, the press officer goes bananas. He wants to know which side the *Globe* thinks it's on. So I tell him, it's not on any side, stupid, it's an objective fact-gathering organization. And he says, yes, but is it objective-for or objective-against? (*Pause*) He may be stupid, but he's not stupid.

GUTHRIE: I've got a present for you.

(GUTHRIE *gets up and walks towards the back of the room where he picks up a pile of newspapers.* WAGNER *doesn't turn to see this.*)

WAGNER: So he spends the briefing attacking the *Globe*—God bless him, it's the only story I've filed this week—and he's in a flat spin trying to make everything fit. At the end, this very smooth guy from Reuters says, 'Let me see if I've got this right. It's not a *political* movement, it's just a lot—or rather *not* a lot—of completely illiterate ivory poachers who've been reading too much Marxist propaganda, and they're all armed with home-made weapons flown by Cuban pilots.'

GUTHRIE: (*Coming back*) Who's the *Globe* special correspondent?

WAGNER: I don't know. I'm famous in Jeddu. Scooped by my own paper. Bloody poaching, that's what it is. It's one of those ivory poachers moonlighting for Hammaker. I'd give

27

anything for a copy of last Sunday's—(GUTHRIE *dumps the newspapers into* WAGNER's *lap*.) Aw, Gigi!

GUTHRIE: I couldn't get them all, just what they had when I changed planes at Karachi. Second lead.

(*The* Sunday Globe *is a respectable English paper. The African story is the second most important story on the front page. The back page is a sports page. The other papers are: the* Sunday Express, *the* Sunday Times, *the* Sunday Mirror, *the* Observer, *the* Sunday Telegraph *and the* News of the World, *and a magazine or two, including* Newsweek.

WAGNER *of course looks at the* Globe *first*.)

GNER: 'A special correspondent'—

GUTHRIE: That's what I said.

WAGNER: What the hell does that mean? Fair old piece. (*He turns the paper to look over the fold*.) Took care of mine anyway—'Richard Wagner adds from Jeddu'—two paragraphs. (*He puts the paper aside*.) Well, well. A world beat and no name on it.

GUTHRIE: A freelance.

WAGNER: They have names. I don't get it.

GUTHRIE: (*Picking up the* Globe) Where is this place?

WAGNER: It's sort of North Wales.

GUTHRIE: What do you mean North Wales?

WAGNER: I've given up on place names here—they all sound like games you play on board ship. If a place isn't called Tombola it's called Housey-housey. The way to look at it is, KC is London, Jeddu is up the A40—Cheltenham—and the Colonel is somewhere in the Welsh hills. (*He has found the inside foreign page of the* Sunday Express *now*.) *Sunday Express* . . . 'The smouldering heart of this coffee-laden, copper-loaded corner of Africa is being ripped apart by the ambitions of a cashiered Colonel whose iron fist, UN observers fear, may turn out to be holding a hammer and sickle. . . .' (*Scornfully*) And a UN dateline, who needs it? (*He tosses that aside and* GUTHRIE *gives him* Newsweek.)

GUTHRIE: *Newsweek*. . . .

WAGNER: Bloody Biedermeier. . . . What's he got to say for himself? 'This time last week Jeddu was a one-horse town on the road from Kamba City to nowhere. Today you can't see the town for cavalry, mainly armoured personnel carriers and a few T-47 tanks. In them thar hills to the north-west, the renegade Colonel Shimbu is given no more chance than Colonel Custer—if only he'd make a stand. Unfortunately, no one can find the Colonel to tell him to stop playing the Indians and it may be that Jeddu is going to wake up one morning with its armoured cars drawn up in a circle.' (*He throws that aside.*) I hate them and their Pulitzer Prizes. All writing and no facts. (*The* Sunday Times.) *Sunday Times.* 'At five minutes past eight on Wednesday morning, an aide-de-camp on the staff of Supreme Commander and President Ginku Mageeba, his uniform distinguished by Christian Dior sunglasses and unbuttoned flies, drove a green and white jeep up to the Princess Alice Bar in downtown Jeddu and commandeered it as the nerve centre of Mageeba's victorious drive against the forces of darkness, otherwise known as the Adoma Liberation Front. The army itself appeared in time for elevenses, and by today the advance had nearly reached the Esso pump three hundred yards up the road towards the enemy.' Very funny. All facts and no news. (*He picks up the* Mirror.) *Mirror.*

GUTHRIE: Nothing.

WAGNER: Well, that's honest anyway. (*The* Observer.) *Observer.* 'Sources close to President Mageeba are conceding that the peasant army of the ALF has the tacit support of the indigenous population of the interior and is able to move unhindered through the Adoma hills.' (*Considers this, nods sagely.*) True. (Sunday Telegraph.) *Sunday Telegraph.* 'Evidence is emerging that the civilian population of the Adoma region has been intimidated into supporting the Russian-equipped rural guerillas of the ALF, but according to army sources, the self-styled Liberation Front is penned up in the Adoma hills.' (*Considers this, nods sagely.*) True.

29

(News of the World—*he only glances at the front page.*) *News of the World.* 'Is this the laziest man in Britain?' I did that one once. Different bloke, mind you.

(WAGNER *turns his attention back to the* Globe, *which* GUTHRIE *has put down. He looks at it glumly. The dog barks. A car is arriving.*)

GUTHRIE: Carson.

WAGNER: (*Still preoccupied with the paper*) I don't think it's anybody who's been around much. It's good stuff but it's too much I-was-there. It's somebody who wants to impress the world and doesn't know that the world isn't impressed by reporters and nobody is impressed by reporters except other reporters—who can work out that you were there without having it rammed down their throats.

(*We have heard car doors.*)

Yeah, I think I've got this one's number—he's not a star, he's a boy scout in an Austin Reed safari suit who somehow got lucky.

(MILNE *enters.* WAGNER's *description is not far off.* WAGNER *hasn't seen him.*)

(*Almost to himself*) Little prick.

MILNE: I say . . .

(GUTHRIE *and* WAGNER *look at him.*)

I say, that wouldn't be a *Sunday Globe*, would it?

(GUTHRIE *and* WAGNER *look at each other.*)

WAGNER: Care to have a look?

MILNE: Not last Sunday's?! I say—*thanks.* . . .

WAGNER: Have you just come with Mr Carson?

MILNE: Yes, that's right. He's just gone up to see his wife.

(WAGNER *gives him the* Globe. MILNE *ignores the front page and thumbs through to the foreign page inside. His disappointment is silent but immense. He tries another page.*)

(*Miserably; scanning the paper*) He's just gone up to see his wife.

(WAGNER *and* GUTHRIE, *especially* WAGNER, *watch him like people watching a play, tensely waiting for* MILNE *to find his story.* MILNE *gives up and closes the paper, giving the front page a casual glance. Then he sees his story and the jolt he gets is audible.* WAGNER *and* GUTHRIE *relax.* MILNE *reads for a few seconds, lost in himself.*)

(*To* WAGNER) Do you need this paper?

WAGNER: No. I'd like you to have it.

MILNE: Thanks awfully. (*Reading again.*) Carson's just gone up to see his wife and boy.

WAGNER: Yes, you said.

MILNE: Are you in mining as well?

WAGNER: As well as what?

    (MILNE *giggles and goes on reading.*)

    Anything interesting in the paper?

    (MILNE *finally puts the paper down.*)

MILNE: Actually, I'm a journalist.

WAGNER: Oh.

MILNE: Actually, I'm on the *Sunday Globe.*

WAGNER: Ah.

MILNE: Well, I'm not actually *on* the *Sunday Globe.*

WAGNER: What are you doing here, actually?

MILNE: I'm covering the rebellion. This is my interview with Colonel Shimbu on the front page.

WAGNER: That's very good. How did you find him?

MILNE: A bit excitable but quite—

WAGNER: (*Hard edge*) How did you find him?

MILNE: Oh. It was a bit of luck really. Some of his men stopped a bus I was on.

WAGNER: What for? Food? Money?

MILNE: No. They give out leaflets and lecture the passengers for a while and let them carry on. But they took me off the bus. I was the only white. That was a month ago before the story broke properly—I mean, the story was there all the time but no one was taking any notice of it, you just heard talk about it. I was in KC so I thought I'd have a recce, and I got kidnapped by this ALF group.

GUTHRIE: Lucky.

MILNE: Yes. I moved around with them for two weeks and finally I persuaded Shimbu he should let his case be properly reported. So he did the interview.

WAGNER: How did you get the story out?

MILNE: He got it out for me.

WAGNER: A pigeon?

MILNE: (*Laughing patronizingly*) A *pigeon*? No, we've got a little beyond that in Fleet Street. He gave it to one of his chaps to take over the border and he posted it for me.

(WAGNER *glances at* GUTHRIE.)

WAGNER: (*Expressionless*) Posted it.

MILNE: To tell you the truth the interview was ten days old but luckily I had Shimbu to myself. By the time the foreign press started to arrive in Kambawe the government got wise and attached the reporters to the army, which sounds promising but it takes away their freedom of movement. On a story like this it's no good at all until the real shooting starts. The story has got to be with the rebels. They should have known that.

(GUTHRIE *smiles at* WAGNER.)

WAGNER: Where was your last job?

MILNE: The *Grimsby Evening Messenger*.

WAGNER: The *Grimsby Evening Messenger*.

MILNE: That's an evening paper in Grimsby, in England. By the way, my name is Jacob Milne.

WAGNER: What are you doing here, Jacob?

MILNE: In this house?

WAGNER: In Africa.

MILNE: Oh. I lost my job in Grimsby.

WAGNER: Yes?

MILNE: My idea was to get myself in on a good foreign story without too much competition. Then I heard that there was this interesting situation developing in Kambawe.

WAGNER: Where did you hear that?

MILNE: In Grimsby. (WAGNER *waits for more.*) In *Time Magazine*.

WAGNER: Ah.

32

MILNE: Incredible how it's worked out. Carson says there's fifty reporters in Jeddu. They've got themselves thoroughly lumbered. There's no story in Jeddu. (*Reading from the Globe.*) '. . . sources close to President Mageeba . . .' Sheer desperation . . . Richard Vahgner. I bet I've made him sick. Well, he's not going to be very pleased about my exclusive, and the awful thing is (*Looking* WAGNER *in the eye.*) *I've got another one.* (*He sees the awful truth in* WAGNER's *eyes.*) Oh, Christ.

WAGNER: Sit down, Jacob.

MILNE: Look, I'm sorry—(*He turns to* GUTHRIE.) are you with—?

GUTHRIE: George Guthrie. Hello.

MILNE: *Guthrie?*—Christ. I thought your Lebanon pictures were just—

WAGNER: Sit down. I'm Dick Wagner. Where have you just come from?

MILNE: The Kaminco Complex—you know—where the Kaminco mines are—I can never get these places right—what's it called?—

GUTHRIE: Ping pong.

MILNE: No.

GUTHRIE: Deck tennis.

WAGNER: Shut up.

MILNE: Malakuangazi. About a hundred and fifty miles north.

GUTHRIE: What's Kaminco?

WAGNER: Kambawe Mining Corporation. Carson's outfit. (*To* MILNE.) How did you get *there*?

MILNE: With the ALF of course. Shimbu captured it this morning. He shelled it and then went in and killed the garrison. That's my story.

(WAGNER *stares at him.*)

WAGNER: Jesus wept.

(CARSON *enters, heading for the study.* WAGNER's *interception is slightly ingratiating.*)

Mr Carson—I'm Richard Wagner, *Sunday Globe.*

CARSON: Yes. Are you helping Jake on his story?

(WAGNER *decides to swallow that.*)

WAGNER: That's right. Fred Hammaker suggested I look you up. Sends his regards. And to Mrs Carson.

CARSON: I'm afraid I've never heard of him. Excuse me.

(*Leaving* WAGNER *looking at the closed study door.*)

GUTHRIE: He's never heard of him.

WAGNER: I'm thinking about it. (*To* MILNE.) How did Hammaker know about Carson?

MILNE: I told him.

GUTHRIE: When you sent your Colonel Shimbu piece.

MILNE: That's right. I thought Jeddu would be the next place I'd have a chance to file. I was right about that, though for the wrong reasons—like everybody else I thought the Colonel was heading this way.

WAGNER: You haven't filed yet?

MILNE: I couldn't. The land cable was cut in the shelling. That's why I came out with Carson. Do you know what Carson has got here?

WAGNER: Seen it. Happy birthday.

MILNE: I knew Geoff Carson slightly. I met him in KC. He spends time in KC and Malakuangazi, it's a dog-leg with Jeddu at the bend, and he's also got a small potash operation just down the road from here—where the helicopter came down. Kaminco is mainly copper but there's some potash and also manganese—

WAGNER: Just get on with it.

MILNE: Well, I interviewed Carson for a background piece when I first arrived in the country. Carson wanted to check his quotes so he gave me his home telex number. I had it in my book. I told Hammaker it was one place he might be able to reach me.

WAGNER: And here you are.

MILNE: With bells on.

(*He takes his 'copy' from his pocket and flourishes it.* WAGNER *takes it from him.*)

WAGNER: Well, you're a bloody idiot. You should have stayed inside and got Carson to carry your story out. He was the pigeon of a lifetime, with his own little helicopter. *Now* how are you going to get back in?

MILNE: Carson said he'd lend me a Kaminco car.

WAGNER: Don't be a clown—no one's going to get into Malakuangazi now without a tank.

GUTHRIE: Why did Shimbu let Carson leave?

MILNE: I don't know. (*Pause—apologetically.*) I thought you meant a real pigeon . . . before. Sorry.

WAGNER: (*To* GUTHRIE) What do you think?

GUTHRIE: (*To* MILNE) Carson's using you for something.

MILNE: Does it matter?

GUTHRIE: Maybe not. I'll come with you.

MILNE: Fine. I never thought I'd be on a story with you.

GUTHRIE: Me neither.

(GUTHRIE *relaxes, having settled his immediate future. He picks up* ALASTAIR's *camera and completes the business of inserting a film.*)

MILNE: How interesting—I always imagined you'd have one of those flashy Japanese jobs with lenses and things. . . .

GUTHRIE: (*Smiles*) There you go.

WAGNER: (*With* MILNE's *story*) Is all this going to stand up? Twelve Mig-17s, three Ilyushin-28s—who told you?

MILNE: I watched them land this morning.

WAGNER: Where did they come from?

MILNE: Yemen. You can see why Shimbu went for Malakuangazi —I should have worked it out. It's not the mine, it's the airstrip. There's no strip at Jeddu for anything bigger than a light plane. In the hills he had to make do with MI-8 choppers to supply him from across the border.

WAGNER: Who flies them?

MILNE: Cubans. It's in there.

WAGNER: Did you actually see a Cuban flying a helicopter?

MILNE: Not exactly—

WAGNER: (*Flaring up*) Listen, Jacob—I know what it's like in

Grimsby. You can say that Cubans have taken over the fishing fleet and next day you say that they haven't, *actually*, and nobody gives a bugger, because it's Grimsby. But this is the *Sunday Globe* and if you say Shimbu's got Cuban pilots you've got to have something better than his word and a Havana cigar—so who says they're Cuban?

MILNE: They do.

WAGNER: (*Pause*) You interviewed them?

MILNE: Not exactly interviewed—they wouldn't let me. We played cards a few times. I was just improving my Spanish. (*His irritation gets the better of him.*) And if you don't mind my saying so, Mr Wagner, you know fuck all about the *Grimsby Evening Messenger*, which is a great deal more important around Grimsby than the *Sunday Globe* is around the globe on any bloody day of the week!

WAGNER: Please call me Dick. This guy with the field battery— did you talk to *him*?

(WAGNER *is referring to* MILNE's *pages.*)

MILNE: Yes.

WAGNER: He spoke English?

MILNE: No, but I know a little Russian—it was my optional language at school.

WAGNER: (*Exasperated*) Tell me something, Jacob—what did you get fired *for*?

MILNE: I didn't exactly get fired. It was after the trouble in the provinces—you know, the strike.

WAGNER: Strike?

MILNE: The provincial reporters' strike. There were several reports in the *Globe*, including one from Grimsby which was not as accurate as one might have wished.

WAGNER: I don't understand. You got fired for going on strike?

MILNE: (*Laughs*) Are you serious?

WAGNER: (*Pause*) Oh no.

MILNE: Yes. It all seems a bit silly out here, doesn't it?

WAGNER: Milne. You're one of those blokes all the fuss was about in . . .

36

MILNE: Grimsby.

WAGNER: (*To* GUTHRIE) Do you see who we've got here? It is the Grimsby scab!

MILNE: I say, that's not very nice.

WAGNER: Is it not?

MILNE: No. I don't keep an abusive vocabulary ready for anyone who acts on different principles.

WAGNER: Oh, acting on principle were you?

MILNE: Yes, I was, as a matter of fact.

WAGNER: Is it your principle to betray your fellow workers when they're in confrontation with management?

(MILNE *can't believe this. He almost laughs.*)

MILNE: Come again?

WAGNER: (*Furious*) Don't patronize *me*, you little berk.

MILNE: I'm sorry—I was just taken aback. I never got used to the way the house Trots fell into the jargon back in Grimsby—I mean, on any other subject, like the death of the novel, or the sex life of the editor's secretary, they spoke ordinary English, but as soon as they started trying to get me to join the strike it was as if their brains had been taken out and replaced by one of those little golf-ball things you get in electric typewriters . . . 'Betrayal' . . . 'Confrontation' . . . 'Management'. . . . My God, you'd need a more supple language than that to describe an argument between two amoebas.

(*But* WAGNER *has already turned away to* GUTHRIE—*well worked up.*)

WAGNER: 'Special Correspondent'! That's why Hammaker didn't give him a by-line! He knew Derek would never have worn it for a minute—

GUTHRIE: What Derek?

WAGNER: Battersby—Derek Battersby—Branch Secretary.

GUTHRIE: Battersby? I went on something with him once . . . bloody useless reporter.

WAGNER: He's bloody good at squeezing the management. They don't always go together.

37

GUTHRIE: Do they *ever* go together?

MILNE: I thought foreign correspondents would find the whole thing a bit parochial.

WAGNER: (*Acidly*) I am not a foreign correspondent. A foreign correspondent is someone who lives in foreign parts and corresponds, usually in the form of essays containing no new facts. I am a fireman. I go to fires. Brighton or Kambawe—they're both out-of-town stories and I cover them the same way. I don't file prose. I file facts. So don't imagine for a moment you've stumbled across a fellow member of the Travellers' Club. To me you're the Grimsby scab. Jacob Milne. Yeah. What happened to the others?

MILNE: What do you mean?

WAGNER: It wasn't just you, was it? Getting out the paper like bob-a-job week?

MILNE: No.

WAGNER: Well I hope they're all making out as stringers up the Limpopo.

MILNE: They're all still on the *Messenger*. After the strike was settled the union expelled us, but the others appealed and got fined. Of course, the union didn't really want to expel me, they expected me to appeal too.

WAGNER: Why didn't you?

MILNE: I was feeling a bit wicked. The *Messenger* isn't officially a closed shop, you see—they'd just got used to having a hundred per cent membership. I gave them a problem.

WAGNER: Smarty-boots.

MILNE: I'm afraid so. But it backfired. By a majority decision they refused to work with me, and it looked as if the paper was going to shut down again, this time because of me.

WAGNER: So the management dumped you. You had to learn the hard way, didn't you? Bosses are bosses, and that's what it's all about, kid.

MILNE: I resigned.

WAGNER: Oh yeah.

MILNE: They refused to sack me.

WAGNER: They just heaved a huge sigh of relief when you went.

MILNE: Possibly.

WAGNER: Well, I hope the experience radicalized you a little. We're working to keep richer men than us richer than us, and nothing's going to change that without worker solidarity.

MILNE: I bet they don't come much more solid than you.

WAGNER: (*Wide-eyed to* GUTHRIE) Did you hear what he just said to me?

MILNE: The *Globe* is losing a million a year, and nobody's getting rich on the *Messenger* either. It's not a private coal-mine sending somebody's son to Eton, it's a limited liability company publishing a reasonably honest and not particularly wonderful local paper in the last two-paper town of its size in the country that began the whole idea of the right to publish, and you'd close it down out of pique—

WAGNER: What are you burbling about?

MILNE: We were called out because the *printers* had got a new deal.

WAGNER: (*High*) Well, there were printers getting more than journalists!

MILNE: Yes, I know, but you make it sound as if the natural order has been overthrown. Fish sing in the streets, rivers run uphill, and the printers are getting more than the journalists. Okay—you're worth more than a printer. But look at some of this—
(*With his hand, or perhaps his foot,* MILNE *spreads the newspapers and the* News of the World *lies in front of him.*) 'Exposed! The Vanishing Vicar of Lovers' Leap! . . .' (*and the* Mirror) 'Sally Smith is a tea lady in a Blackpool engineering works, but it was the way she filled those C-cups which got our cameraman all stirred up!' It's *crap*. And it's written by grown men earning maybe ten thousand a year. If I was a printer, I'd look at some of the stuff I'm given to print, and I'd ask myself what is supposed to be so special about the people who write it—is that radical enough for you—Dick?

39

(*The feeling is that* WAGNER *might actually hit him. Before we can find out whether he would have done or not, the study door opens and* CARSON *comes out, head bent over a sheet of telex paper in his hands. He comes out reading.*)

CARSON: 'Onpass Milne. Congratulations Shimbu interview worldwide interest. Hammaker.'

(*He hands this to* MILNE.)

MILNE: Oh . . . thanks.

CARSON: Sorry I had to leave you so long.

(CARSON *nods at* GUTHRIE.)

GUTHRIE: George Guthrie.

CARSON: George. (*They shake hands.*) . . . and . . .

WAGNER: Dick Wagner.

CARSON: Good. Geoff is my name. Should we have a beer? Or would you prefer something stronger?

GUTHRIE: Beer is fine.

CARSON: Dick?

WAGNER: Thank you.

CARSON: Sure you wouldn't rather have a scotch?

WAGNER: Much rather. Thanks.

(CARSON *looks again at* GUTHRIE.)

GUTHRIE: No—beer is fine.

CARSON: Jake?

(MILNE *seems to be still reading the telex.*)

MILNE: Yes?

CARSON: Beer or scotch?

MILNE: Yes—fine.

(CARSON *orders the drinks on the house phone.*)

CARSON: (*To* MILNE) You can try London now if you like.

WAGNER: We're very grateful to you . . . Geoff . . . most grateful.

CARSON: (*To* MILNE) By the way you've got the spare room.

MILNE: Thank you.

(CARSON *leaves.*)

WAGNER: I want to use that thing.

MILNE: How do you get London anyway?

WAGNER: You may be wasting your time.

MILNE: Why?

GUTHRIE: You're kidding.

WAGNER: No, I'm an officer of the *Globe* chapel.

GUTHRIE: That doesn't make it your responsibility.

WAGNER: That's right. Let Hammaker fight it out with Battersby at branch level.

MILNE: What is this?

WAGNER: (*By way of answer*) 'Onpass Battersby. Must protest employment of special correspondent Milne, non-member ex-Grimsby.' Nothing personal. Send the piece. I'm not stopping you.

MILNE: Thanks a lot.

GUTHRIE: You *are* kidding.

WAGNER: Watch me. (*He goes to the study door and then invites* MILNE.) Watch me?

(MILNE *goes into the study with* WAGNER, *who shuts the door.* GUTHRIE *takes a camera out of the camera bag and hangs it round his neck.* CARSON *returns.*)

CARSON: Ruth's just coming down.

GUTHRIE: Okay if I take a picture?

CARSON: What for?

GUTHRIE: I don't know. Can I?

CARSON: I suppose there's no harm.

(GUTHRIE *gets ready to take pictures, and is taking them over the next few moments until* RUTH's *entrance.*)

GUTHRIE: How can you get back into that place?

CARSON: Malakuangazi? There's no way you can get me back. I was lucky to get out.

GUTHRIE: I mean . . .

CARSON: Oh . . . How can *you* . . .

GUTHRIE: Me and Jake.

CARSON: Jake asked me to help him.

GUTHRIE: Can you?

CARSON: Mageeba will have got his armour up there. You can't just stroll through.

GUTHRIE: What then?

CARSON: We'll see.

GUTHRIE: Do you know Shimbu?

CARSON: Yes.

GUTHRIE: Why did he let you out? (*Pause*) I wondered if you were some kind of . . . I don't mean messenger—

CARSON: Emissary.

GUTHRIE: Yes.

(CARSON *doesn't reply.* GUTHRIE *takes pictures. The telephone rings.* GUTHRIE *had just finished but this gives him a different sort of picture to take and he takes some while* CARSON *is on the phone.* CARSON *does hardly any talking, much more listening. What he says isn't audible anyway.*

Behind CARSON, *on phone, and* GUTHRIE, WAGNER *comes out of the study, closing the door behind him just as* RUTH *enters from within the house. When they see each other they pause, looking at each other.* WAGNER *smiles.*

CARSON *hangs up and turns and sees them.* FRANCIS *enters with a tray of drinks, beers and scotches.*)

CARSON: Ah, darling—have you met?

RUTH: No, we haven't. Mr Guthrie told me you were expected . . . (*Offering her hand.*) Mr . . . Strauss . . . ? (*She takes a scotch off the tray.*) Thank you, Francis. (*Her manner is amused, relaxed.*)

WAGNER: Wagner.

RUTH: Wagner. Exactly. I knew it was Richard.

WAGNER: How nice to meet you, Mrs Carson.

(FRANCIS *is moving around and the drinks are being taken off his tray.*)

CARSON: We're Geoff and Ruth to everyone around here. (*He takes a beer off the tray.*) Isn't that right, Francis?

FRANCIS: Yes sir, Mr Carson.

WAGNER: Ruth, then.

RUTH: And I'll call you Richard.

WAGNER: Most people call me Dick.

RUTH: I'm not terribly fond of Dick.

42

WAGNER: You could have fooled me.

(*Their position in the room has enabled him to say this evenly.*)

RUTH: Well, that's that settled. Why don't we sit down?

'RUTH': And fasten your seatbelts. I'm having no more nonsense from the pride of Wagga Wagga.

GUTHRIE: (*To* FRANCIS, *but for* RUTH's *benefit; taking his beer off the tray*) Thank you, sir. . . .

(FRANCIS *leaves.*)

RUTH: Where's the other chap? The one who came with you?

CARSON: Jacob Milne.

WAGNER: He's in there trying to raise London. Do you know London, Ruth?

RUTH: Oh, rather. Good old London, eh? . . . the red buses scattering the pigeons in Trafalgar Square. . . .

CARSON: Yes, indeed.

RUTH: Covent Garden porters with baskets of fruit and veg piled on their heads, threading their way among the flower girls and professors of linguistics.

CARSON: All gone now.

RUTH: Flexing their native wit against the inimitable banter of the pearly kings. . . . The good old London bobby keeping a fatherly eye on the children feeding the beefeaters outside Buckingham Palace . . .

CARSON: Oh, all right.

RUTH: . . . giving himself a glancing blow with his riot shield every time a tourist asks him the time.

(*She turns her wrist to look at her watch and staggers back from an imaginary blow to the forehead.*)

CARSON: Don't be a rotter. (*To* WAGNER.) How is London really?

GUTHRIE: Don't ask him—he's a bloody colonial, knows nothing.

(*Deep pause.* RUTH *is amused.* CARSON *is forgiving.* GUTHRIE *apologetic.* WAGNER *helps out.*)

WAGNER: It's quite true about me. When I first arrived in London I thought Fleet Street was between the Strand and Trafalgar Square. I was working from a Monopoly board.

RUTH: We play Monopoly with Alastair.

43

CARSON: Do we?

RUTH: On Boxing Day. As far as I remember Fleet Street was yellow and rather cheap. Is that right, Dick?

WAGNER: Not necessarily. Leicester Square and Coventry Street were yellow. To be fair you'd never confuse Fleet Street with Soho on the ground, you never saw anything so sleazy —the whole place has given itself over to crude titillation and eye-catching junk.

RUTH: And how about Soho?

WAGNER: (*Catching up*) Soho. You're a caution.

RUTH: Where are you from, George?

GUTHRIE: London Wall. In the City. Of course, it's all been knocked down now. Bloody shame.

CARSON: Yes, indeed.

GUTHRIE: You should see it now. Do you know St Paul's?

RUTH: I've heard of it.

CARSON: Actually, Ruth was born in London.

GUTHRIE: Really? Well, you wouldn't know it now. When were you last there?

RUTH: Friday.

GUTHRIE: (*Pause*) I think I'll just sit and drink my beer.

CARSON: (*To* RUTH) You're a rotter.

(*The telephone rings and he gets up to answer it. Again he does more listening than talking.*)

RUTH: I'm a rotter, George. I'm a frightful rotter. I was picking up Allie from prep school, his first term at Ascot Heath.

(ALASTAIR *comes in wearing pyjamas and dressing gown and slippers.*)

Hello, darling, your mummy's a rotter. Have you come to say goodnight?

ALASTAIR: (*Outraged*) Goodnight? I haven't even had supper.

RUTH: Well, go and see Winnie, she'll have it ready.

ALASTAIR: I want to talk to Mr Guthrie.

RUTH: Mr Guthrie will come and see you, won't you, George?

GUTHRIE: Never fear.

(*He stands and yawns.*)

ALASTAIR: Will you come and see me in my room?

GUTHRIE: Promise.

RUTH: So will I. Say goodnight to Mr Wagner.

ALASTAIR: Goodnight.

WAGNER: Goodnight, Alastair.

ALASTAIR: You won't forget, George?

RUTH: Mr Guthrie to you—hop it.

> (ALASTAIR *goes*. GUTHRIE *gets comfortable*.)
>
> Oh dear, he's taken rather a fancy to George. Next thing, he'll want to be a journalist when he grows up. What is a mother to do?
>
> (CARSON *hangs up the phone*.)
>
> Should I tell him it'll send him blind, and risk psychological damage?

CARSON: (*Leaving the room*) Darling, these gentlemen may not be used to your sense of humour. (*Calling*) Allie!

RUTH: Well I'm going to *need* a sense of humour if Alastair's going to go around the house putting his foot in the doors and asking impertinent questions. Perhaps I'll get him a reporter doll for Christmas. Wind it up and it gets it wrong. (*She seems in high good humour*.) What does it say when you press its stomach? Come on, Dick!

WAGNER: I name the guilty man.

RUTH: (*Laughs*) Very good.

> (CARSON *comes back and takes his place*. RUTH *gets up to replenish her glass*.)
>
> Yes, that's a question which has loomed large in my life— who's the guilty man? Until Geoffrey of course. Geoffrey is entirely blameless.

CARSON: Steady on, Ruth.

WAGNER: Who is the guilty man this time, Geoff?

'RUTH': Don't get cheeky, Wagner. He's not stupid.

WAGNER: There's always a guilty man . . .

'RUTH': Wagner—

WAGNER: . . . isn't there? Who do I name?

'RUTH': . . . for God's sake, Wagner, there are rules—

WAGNER: Shimbu or Mageeba?

CARSON: Oh. . . .

'RUTH': Nice one. . . .

CARSON: Depends which paper you read, doesn't it?

(RUTH *takes her drink and sits apart from the men.*)

WAGNER: What did the President have to say?

CARSON: Are you interviewing me, Dick?

WAGNER: Is that all right?

CARSON: No, it isn't.

WAGNER: Off the record, then.

'RUTH': Tell him to bugger off.

WAGNER: No attribution.

'RUTH': I'll tell him. Elizabeth Taylor in *Elephant Walk* . . .
(*Shouts*) 'Get out of this house! This is no longer Geoffrey
Carson's bachelor quarters, I'm his beautiful bride from
England, and I'm sick of all you hooligans playing bicycle
polo in my sitting-room!'
(CARSON *realizes that* GUTHRIE *has fallen asleep holding his
beer glass.* CARSON *goes over and gently takes the glass out of*
GUTHRIE's *hands.*)

CARSON: George tells me he'd like to get into Malakuangazi.

WAGNER: We both would.

CARSON: What about Jake?

WAGNER: Jake is a freelance. I'm the *Globe*'s man on this
story.

CARSON: He did well.

WAGNER: Yes, he did well. He had some luck.

CARSON: Was that it?

WAGNER: Okay, but now it's up to me to go where I can get
ahead of the competition. There'll be a lot of journalists
with the same idea.

CARSON: They haven't got a hope. The army won't let them
through.

WAGNER: Can you help?

CARSON: Yes. I can give you a car, a driver who speaks the
lingo, and a pass signed by the President.

46

WAGNER: My God, what am I doing for you?

CARSON: Colonel Shimbu didn't let me go for old times' sake. I was taking a message. You'll be taking the reply.

WAGNER: You were taking a message from Shimbu?

CARSON: Yes.

WAGNER: To President Mageeba?

CARSON: I didn't say that.

WAGNER: Well, what are you saying?

CARSON: Use your imagination.

WAGNER: Unprofessional. What *I* use has to check out.

CARSON: Well, I'm flying down to KC. I'll be back in the morning, early, with a letter and the pass.

WAGNER: Signed by Mageeba.

CARSON: That's it.

WAGNER: And the letter too? (*Pause*) Just say yes—what's the matter? Has Shimbu offered a deal?

CARSON: Come on, Dick. Well, you can assume I wouldn't ask you if I thought there'd be a war going on.

WAGNER: Why a journalist?

CARSON: Who else would want to go? I was thinking of Jake.

WAGNER: No. How long is the drive?

CARSON: About five hours. Lunch in Malakuangazi.

WAGNER: Friday lunch. Twenty-four hours to get back here and file. That's nice going if the Colonel cooperates.

CARSON: It might be better if Jake went. Shimbu likes him.

WAGNER: Shimbu will like me. I'm very popular.

RUTH: I've always wanted to meet a popular journalist. I mean socially, I don't mean under one's bed or outside the law courts. One is not normally introduced to journalists. I mention that as a matter of circumstance, not as a piece of social etiquette. Though, of course, it is that, too.

CARSON: I *thought* you were being unnaturally silent.

WAGNER: You don't much care for the media, do you, Ruth?

RUTH: The media. It sounds like a convention of spiritualists.

CARSON: Ruth has mixed feelings about reporters.

RUTH: No, I haven't. I despise them. Not foreign correspondents,

of course—or the gardening notes. The ones in between.
I'm sure you know what I mean.

WAGNER: You've met one or two, have you?

RUTH: Under the bed, outside the law courts. . . . But don't
imagine that I despise them because of any injury done to
me—on the contrary I looked jolly nice in my divorce hat,
and being on the front page of four morning newspapers did
my reputation nothing but good in my part of Highgate—
'Hasn't she done well?' And even the indignities with which
the whole saga began . . . well, there are worse things than
being pursued across Shropshire by the slavering minions
of a philistine press lord; in fact, it brought Geoffrey and
me closer together. I loved him for the way he out-drove
them in his Jaguar, and it wasn't his fault at all that the
early morning tea in our hideaway hotel was brought in by
a Fleet Street harpie in a tweeny . . . no, no, it isn't that. It
isn't even—or anyway not entirely—the way it was written
up, or rather snapped together in that Lego-set language
they have, so that poor Geoffrey's wife, a notably hard-
boiled zoologist who happens to breed rare parakeets, and
who incautiously admitted to a reporter that, yes she would
like Geoff to give me up, and yes, she would have him back,
was instantly dubbed Heartbreak Parrot Woman In Plea for
Earl's Brother. Earl's brother. That's the bit. Of all the
husbands who ran off with somebody's wife that week,
Geoffrey qualified because he had a measly title and if the
right three-hundred people went down on the Royal Yacht
he'd be Duke of Bognor. *Has anyone ever bothered to find out
whether anybody really cares?* The populace and the popular
press. What a grubby symbiosis it is. Which came first?
The rhinoceros or the rhinoceros bird?

WAGNER: Sex, money and a title; and the parrots didn't harm it
either. I remember you now—just. The beginning of the
gossip-column war. Nick Webster was allowed thirty
thousand pounds a year for tip-off money. Thought he was
the scourge of privilege. Thought the paper was behind

him. Don't you love it? If someone had convinced the paper that the AB readership had gone over to astronomy, Nick would have found himself on the roof with a telescope.

(*The study door opens.*)

MILNE: Dick! I got a line!

(*The study door closes.* WAGNER *gets up to go.*)

WAGNER: Yeah—I agree with you. Newspapers have got more important things to do.

(WAGNER *goes out into the study, closing the door behind him.*)

CARSON: You're riding him a little hard, aren't you? Is anything the matter?

(*The phone rings.* CARSON *goes over to it and is using it during this scene.*)

'RUTH': Matter? Matter? What do you mean, matter? What could possibly be . . .

CARSON: Nothing wrong, is there?

'RUTH': Wrong? How do you mean, wrong? Why should anything be—

CARSON: What's up?

'RUTH': *Up?*

CARSON: (*Into phone*) Carson. (*Pause; turns back to her.*) Eh, Ruth?

'RUTH': Actually, Geoffrey, yes. Matter, wrong, up.

CARSON: (*Into phone*) Well, tell him it's me. Tell him I've got a courier fixed up. A journalist.

'RUTH': Geoffrey, there's something I have to tell you.

CARSON: (*Into phone*) Well, who else would want to go?

'RUTH': Geoffrey, darling, when I was in London I did something rather silly.

CARSON: (*Into phone*) All right—I'll be here. (*He hangs up, but holds on to the phone, trailing its lead, coming back.*) If this thing comes off . . . (*He looks round vaguely.*) Where are they going to sit?

'RUTH': This is going to amuse you terribly, Geoffrey—

CARSON: Aren't you talking to me, Ruth?

RUTH: (*Turning to him*) I'm sorry I'm a rotten wife.

CARSON: You're not a rotten wife. I've had one of those.

RUTH: At least she was good at *something*.

CARSON: Parrots.

RUTH: (*Unjoking*) Yes—parrots. That's something. Parrot woman. You respected her for that at least.

CARSON: What's the matter?

RUTH: (*Insisting*) You must have been impressed.

(CARSON *studies her warily for a moment; and handles it.*)

CARSON: Well, if someone comes up to you at a party, bites your finger and says: 'Who's a pretty boy, then?' it makes an impression. (*He wins a grimace-smile, and encourages her.*) Come on. . . .

RUTH: That's the disadvantage of being carried off as a virgin; it was years before I discovered I was brighter than most of the people I met. I mean, I could run the mines, Geoffrey, if I knew anything about mining. You know what I mean?

CARSON: Well, you nearly got your chance.

RUTH: I know, I'm a pig; you could have been dead today and I can't take it as seriously as my trite sense of failure. Oh, damn. I had a bad moment in London. Cried buckets.

CARSON: Why, what happened?

RUTH: Allie didn't have Cash's name tapes.

CARSON: (*Pause*) What?

RUTH: He was supposed to have Cash's name tapes sewn into every bloody gym-sock. He was the only one without. Matron said, didn't he write to you? He was told to write home for Cash's name tapes.

CARSON: Well, why didn't he?

RUTH: Exactly. Buckets.

CARSON: Well . . . it's not exactly *The Winslow Boy*.

RUTH: I bet the Winslow boy had Cash's name tapes at least. (*A sniff, the nearest she gets to a tear; then climbing back. . . .*) I could tell by the way Matron looked me over she'd *read* about sundowners and wife-swapping in the White Highlands. But, then, I was never meant to go over big with school matrons. I was meant to be one of those women

50

who halt the cutlery as they pass through hotel dining-rooms on the first night of the holiday . . . tits-first to the table through the ack-ack of teeny-weeny diamond engagement rings. (*Pause*) I'm in the wrong movie, I think. I should be in *Ruth Carson*. Speakeasy queen.

CARSON: I really don't know what you're talking about half the time.

RUTH: And that's the half I do out loud.

CARSON: (*Confirmation*) There you are. (*Pause*) Do you want a change? (*Pause. The phone rings in his hands.*) Sorry. (*Apologetically*) Got to save the country. (*Into phone.*) Carson . . .
(*He takes the phone back across the room away from her, doing more listening than talking.*)
(*Into phone*) Yes, sir. . . . That's right. . . .

'RUTH': Yes, I wouldn't mind a change, actually, Geoffrey darling. Just a thought, you know. I had this cowardly idea —delusion, I mean—that I might change everything in one go by the pointless confession of an unimportant adultery.

CARSON: (*Into phone*) Fine—go ahead.
(RUTH *lights a cigarette.*)

'RUTH': I forget the title. (*Pause; loudly.*) I have brought shame on the house of Carson! Yes! It's Dick! He took advantage of me, Geoffrey! I fought it, my God how I fought it! But I couldn't help myself!
(CARSON *listening at the phone, half turns with his free hand stretched out towards her, his fingers ready to receive a lit cigarette.*)
Don't shoot, Geoffrey!
(*She puts her cigarette between his fingers. During the following,* CARSON *once or twice interjects,* 'Yes, sir', 'Very well'. . . .)
(*Casually*) By the way, Geoffrey, I let Wagner take me to bed in London, in the Royal Garden Hotel, view over Kensington High Street, chosen for its proximity to the Embassy, in the visa section of which I met him while he was fixing his papers. I was fixing Alastair's. 'Going out to

51

Kambawe?' 'Actually, I live there.' 'How interesting. I'm
going out for the *Sunday Globe*. I say, you couldn't spare
the time for a chat, could you?—spot of lunch—dinner—
drinks—nightcap—and so on.' And so on. I believe it's
called de-briefing. Not half bad either, though not as good
as he thinks. Next day I picked up Allie and flew home.
(CARSON *hangs up the phone.*)

CARSON: It's on.

'RUTH': I didn't blame Wagner at all, 'til he showed up here
looking for a second helping. I thought I let him off lightly.
That man is not a gentleman. Thinks I hop into bed with
strange men because I hopped into bed with a strange man.
(*Pause*) I'm sorry.

CARSON: Are you listening, Ruth?

RUTH: I'm sorry—

CARSON: I've told Allie to get dressed.

RUTH: What?

CARSON: He can stay with the Krebs for a couple of days. I
don't want him here.

RUTH: Is it on, then?

CARSON: Looks like it. You really ought to go, too. I trust
Mageeba less than I trust Shimbu, and I don't trust
Shimbu.

RUTH: Do you want me to go with Allie?

CARSON: No. I don't.

(RUTH *kisses him. Nothing too special.*)

RUTH: Then I'll stay.

(WAGNER, *re-entering from the study, almost catches this.*)

WAGNER: Sorry.

CARSON: All right.

(WAGNER *would have retired, but now closes the study door and
comes forward.*)

I'll go and see how Allie's getting on.

(CARSON *goes.*)

WAGNER: Is it safe to come in?

RUTH: Why not?

(RUTH *goes to the drinks shelf, and pours the remainder of a bottle of J and B into a glass for herself. It makes a large double scotch.*)

WAGNER: I had the feeling I was bad news.

RUTH: Bad news? Whatever gave you that idea? I name this ship *Titanic*—(*She smashes the neck of the empty bottle on the marble shelf.*)—long may she sail.

(*She drops the rest of the bottle into the bin at her feet, then picks up the house-phone.*)

Francis, we're out of scotch. (*She turns to* WAGNER.)

WAGNER: You seemed to find me agreeable enough in London.

RUTH: And you thought I might find you just as agreeable in Jeddu, eh? That's something I forgive. It's crass but I forgive it. And just in case finding-you-agreeable-enough is supposed to be Australian understatement for blowing the lid off my billabong, let me tell you something, Wagner— if I had fancied you *at all* when you chatted me up in the visa office, I would have run a mile. That's what we honourable ladies with decent husbands do—didn't you know that? Every now and again we meet a man who attracts us, and we run a mile. I let you take me to dinner because there was no danger of going to bed with you. And then because there was no danger of going to bed with you a second time, I went to bed with you. A lady, if surprised by melancholy, might go to bed with a chap, once; or a thousand times if consumed by passion. But twice, Wagner, *twice* . . . a lady might think she'd been taken for a tart.

(*Pause*)

WAGNER: What is it about *me* that makes *you* think that I would desert the international camaraderie of the Princess Alice bar in downtown Jeddu, and drive *all this way* across the smouldering heart of this copper-loaded corner of Africa, just to find out if *you* are still putting yourself *about*? Eh? What is it *about* me that makes you think that I don't know the difference between a woman on her fifth drink in a hotel room three thousand miles from home, and a woman

ordering a fresh bottle from the servant-quarters under her
own roof, even when it's the same woman? Did you think
that the twin social handicaps of Australia and journalism
left me so unprepared for your mystery that I got culture-
shock when you took your Harrods knickers off? What is it
about *you* that makes you think it's likely? All I can see is a
fairly interesting woman with a very boring problem: you
don't know what you're doing here, and the days go very
slowly. But I didn't come here to brighten up your day.
This is a cable I got from my editor. (*He gives her the cable.*)
I didn't know what it meant, but it turned out to mean that
if I got off my backside I would find a private telex four
miles down the road from a post office which has only just
given up tom-toms; and I can't see anything in this room
as beautiful as that telex. I am in love with it. I would have
come on my hands and knees. Because I'm known for doing
two things well: I can usually find out what's going on in a
place while I am in it, and I can usually find a way to get
the story back to my office in time to catch the first edition.
It's not so much to be proud about, and if I fail nothing
happens—not to Kambawe, not to the paper—but such as
it is it is my pride, and what I want to know is, what are
you so proud of that you can look at your life and sneer at
mine? I mean, what is the secret of your success?
(*Both still. Pause.*)

RUTH: If you're waiting for me to say ouch, you're going to get
cramp. I don't share with strangers. All you're saying is,
'Who do you think you are?' Well, I don't have to be
anybody. So far, the only points you've scored are for not
knowing a Marks and Spencer knicker when you see it.
And as for that, don't tell me it never crossed your mind
you might get lucky again.

WAGNER: As you'll remember, it wasn't that good. If it reminded
you you were in love with your husband, that's good news
for the world.

RUTH: I'm not in love with anybody. I just like some people

54

a great deal more than I like others, and I like Geoffrey a
great deal more than I like you. Is that all right?

WAGNER: Yes, that's fine.

RUTH: Good. (*She gives him back the cable.*) Happy birthday.
(FRANCIS *enters with a fresh bottle of scotch.* ALASTAIR *comes in
dressed to travel.*)
Thank you, Francis. Come to give me a kiss, Allie?

ALASTAIR: No—I want my camera.

RUTH: Be quick then.
(RUTH *goes out.* ALASTAIR *goes to where* GUTHRIE *is sleeping.
He kneels down and whispers to him.*)

ALASTAIR: Mr Guthrie . . .

WAGNER: Don't wake him. I'll find your camera.

ALASTAIR: He said he'd show me how it works.

WAGNER: He put a film in for you. (*He finds the camera where*
GUTHRIE *had been sitting.*) Here you are.

ALASTAIR: Oh . . . gosh, thanks. It's my dad's old camera really.

WAGNER: I say, I thought you were going to bed.

ALASTAIR: Daddy's taking me to Kamba City.

WAGNER: Why's that?

ALASTAIR: I'm going to stay with Krebs. Do you know him?

WAGNER: No.

ALASTAIR: He lives in KC. He's my friend.

WAGNER: Oh.

ALASTAIR: I bet you don't know who my dad is going to see. I'll
give you a hundred guesses.

WAGNER: Father Christmas.

ALASTAIR: No.

WAGNER: Mohammed Ali.

ALASTAIR: Getting warm.

WAGNER: President Mageeba.

ALASTAIR: He told you.

WAGNER: Do you know the President?

ALASTAIR: No, I'm too young. That's why daddy's sending me to
KC. He doesn't want me here when the President comes.

WAGNER: (*Pause*) When is the President coming here?

55

ALASTAIR: Tomorrow night, probably. Don't tell daddy I know it's him—he just said it was somebody coming.

WAGNER: And who told you it was the President, then?

ALASTAIR: My mum.

(*Off-stage* CARSON *calls 'Allie!'*)

WAGNER: Don't worry, I won't tell him.

(CARSON *enters, followed by* RUTH *carrying a small suitcase and a bag of toys.*)

(*With camera*) You have to guess how far it is—you turn this, you see—three feet—six feet—and that's infinity, which means as far as you can see.

CARSON: Come on, Allie, into the car. (*To* WAGNER, *as Allie goes to the door with* RUTH.) Allie was going to visit a pal in KC —so I'm taking him now—

WAGNER: I see.

CARSON: Might as well. Two birds with one stone.

WAGNER: What a childhood, eh?

CARSON: Yes. He's quite used to helicopters.

WAGNER: Yes, he was saying. Well, I hope everything goes well for you.

CARSON: See you in the morning.

WAGNER: Thanks, Geoff.

(CARSON *goes out.* WAGNER *stands still, thinking, and listens to the sounds of farewell, the car doors slamming, the car leaving.* WAGNER *is tense, and then he gives an inarticulate cry of triumph and punches his fist through the air like a goal-scorer. He moves quickly to* GUTHRIE *and slaps his hands together by* GUTHRIE'S *ear, calls his name, and wakes him unceremoniously.* GUTHRIE *comes awake, and stands up in the same moment, talking.*)

GUTHRIE: I'm fine—I'm fine—where are we going?

(WAGNER *is as high as a kite.*)

WAGNER: I'm going back to the hotel. Need the car. (GUTHRIE *relapses into the chair.*) Keys! Listen, you're going to Malakuangazi, you and Jake, in the morning.

GUTHRIE: I should bloody think so.

56

WAGNER: I've got you a car, a driver and a pass, and I've arranged a cease-fire. The *Globe* never sleeps.

GUTHRIE: (*Bitterly*) I know.

WAGNER: I'll cover this end.

(RUTH *returns to the room.*)

RUTH: George—poor George—when did you last sleep in a bed?

GUTHRIE: I was just pretending to be asleep. It's an old photographer's trick.

RUTH: Oh yes, I'm sure.

GUTHRIE: I promised to go and see Alastair—

RUTH: Oh dear—you've missed him—

GUTHRIE: Missed him?

WAGNER: I gave him the camera. You'll see him next time. (*To* RUTH.) I'm taking George to the hotel.

RUTH: There's room in the dorm. Geoffrey arranged it.

WAGNER: Well, that *would* be better. It's going to be quite an early start.

RUTH: We eat early.

GUTHRIE: Yes, thanks. I'll get my stuff out of the car.

(GUTHRIE *goes out.*)

I hope you don't mind sharing a room?

WAGNER: You're a sport, Mrs Carson, but let's just be friends.

RUTH: Bastard.

WAGNER: I made an excuse and left.

(WAGNER *is leaving but* MILNE *comes out of the study holding a piece of telex.* MILNE *doesn't see* RUTH.)

MILNE: Dick, I've got your reply—

WAGNER: What?

MILNE: (*Slightly embarrassed*) The reply to your, um, protest . . .

WAGNER: Oh yes? From Battersby?

MILNE: No. From Hammaker.

WAGNER: Well, what does it say?

MILNE: 'Onpass Wagner. Upstick protest arsewards. Hammaker.'

WAGNER: This is Jacob Milne. He'll be making the trip with George.

MILNE: Oh—how do you do?

RUTH: How do you do?

WAGNER: You're staying the night here, Jake, leaving early tomorrow. Geoffrey will fill you in.

MILNE: Fine.

WAGNER: If the land-line is still out, one of you'd better get back here to file early Saturday to be safe. Either give Gigi your copy or bring his film out.

MILNE: Okay. Don't worry. What will you do?

WAGNER: Best I can. (*To* RUTH.) Thanks for everything. (*To* MILNE.) See you.

MILNE: No hard feelings?

WAGNER: It was your story anyway. (*He's going but a thought strikes him.*) Why did you choose the *Globe*?

MILNE: Well, Hammaker started on the *Messenger*. Didn't you know that?

WAGNER: No, I didn't.

MILNE: Yes. He's famous in Grimsby.

WAGNER: (*Smiles*) I bet.

(WAGNER *goes.*)

RUTH: What was that about no hard feelings?

MILNE: Dick isn't very happy about the *Globe* using me. He's a strong union man.

RUTH: And you're not.

MILNE: It's not that. It's just that I think journalism is . . . special. Dick thinks I'm naïve about newspapers.

RUTH: And you're not?

MILNE: Do you think I am?

RUTH: I haven't really had time to form an opinion.

MILNE: He thinks the *Globe* is a million packets of journalism manufactured every week by businessmen using journalists for their labour.

RUTH: That *is* what the *Globe* is.

MILNE: No, it's not. A free press, free expression—it's the last line of defence for all the other freedoms.

RUTH: I've formed an opinion.

58

MILNE: (*Laughs*) No, really—

RUTH: Why don't you sit down?

MILNE: No, thanks. I'm still—you know . . .

RUTH: Would you like a drink?

MILNE: No, thanks.

RUTH: (*Holding out her empty glass*) Would you be good enough . . . ? Straight scotch.

MILNE: (*Taking the glass*) Of course.

(RUTH *gets up*.)

'RUTH': Watch yourself, Tallulah.

(*The scene moves now into the moonlit garden*.)

MILNE: (*Doing the drink*) Dick wants union membership to be a licence to practise. 'This man has been judged fit.'

(*He joins* RUTH *and gives her the scotch. She goes further into the garden and* MILNE *follows her*.)

Like doctors and lawyers, I suppose.

RUTH: Nothing wrong with that. Otherwise you'd have lawyers amputating the wrong leg.

'RUTH': You're giggling. Shut up.

RUTH: Mining engineers have the same sort of thing, I believe. Professional standards. Don't you think they're important?

MILNE: Oh, yes. But nothing could be further from Dick's mind. The fact is nobody's going to be drummed out of the NUJ for professional incompetence—persistent inaccuracy or illiteracy or getting drunk at the Lord Mayor's dinner. On the contrary it's the union which is going to keep them in their jobs. No, what Dick wants is a *right-thinking press*—one that thinks like him.

RUTH: So what? You'd like a right-thinking press, too. One that thinks like you.

MILNE: Sure I would, but I don't intend to get it by blacklisting *him*.

RUTH: Perhaps you should.

MILNE: Think about it.

RUTH: (*Pause*) Yes, quite.

'RUTH': Clarissa, who's this rather interesting young man?

59

MILNE: Once you establish the machinery it'll be there for someone else to use. Drum you out if you're too left-wing, or not left-wing enough, or the wrong colour, or something.

RUTH: Well, it would be up to you, wouldn't it? Everybody's got a vote.

MILNE: Everybody who's allowed in would have a vote, yes.

RUTH: You're an alarmist, Jacob. On the whole people behave responsibly.

MILNE: On the whole because their behaviour is observed. Reported.

RUTH: You're a cynic.

MILNE: Me?

RUTH: No, that can't be right.

MILNE: It wouldn't be like the Law Society or the BMA.

RUTH: It would in principle. If some group got control of the Law Society, they'd be just as free to have only right-thinking solicitors. What then?

MILNE: Then you'd *really* need a free press, otherwise you may never find out about it. That's the whole point. No matter how imperfect things are, if you've got a free press everything is correctable, and without it everything is concealable.

RUTH: I'm with you on the free press. It's the newspapers I can't stand.

MILNE: (*Laughs*) You don't have to tell me, I know it better than you—the celebration of inanity, and the way real tragedy is paraphrased into an inflationary spiral of hackneyed melodramas—Beauty Queen In Tug-Of-Love Baby Storm . . . Tug-Of-Love Baby Mum In Pools Win . . . Pools Man In Beauty Queen Drug Quiz. I *know*. It's the price you pay for the part that matters.

'RUTH': I like that one who's doing all the talking.

MILNE: It's not easy to defend, but it's mainly attacked for the wrong reasons. People think that rubbish-journalism is produced by men of discrimination who are vaguely

60

ashamed of truckling to the lowest taste. But it's not. It's produced by people doing their best work. Proud of their expertise with a limited number of cheap devices to put a shine on the shit. Sorry. I know what I'm talking about because I started off like that, admiring it, trying to be *that good*, looking up to Fleet Street stringers, London men sometimes, on big local stories. I thought it was great. Some of the best times in my life have been spent sitting in a clapped-out Ford Consul outside a suburban house with a packet of Polos and twenty Players, waiting to grab a bereaved husband or a footballer's runaway wife who might be good for one front page between oblivion and oblivion. I felt part of a privileged group, inside society and yet outside it, with a licence to scourge it and a duty to defend it, night and day, the street of adventure, the fourth estate. And the thing is— I was dead right. That's what it was, and I *was* part of it because it's indivisible. Junk journalism is the evidence of a society that has got at least one thing right, that there should be nobody with the power to dictate where responsible journalism begins. (*Pause*) I'm sorry.
I'm not usually so wound up. It's been an amazing day. I was the only reporter in Malakuangazi, you know. I mean, that story I sent over, it's probably the best story I'll ever get in my life.

RUTH: You must be tired.

MILNE: Not a bit.

RUTH: Hungry?

MILNE: Starving.

RUTH: Then let's eat.

MILNE: I'm sorry I talked so much.

RUTH: No. I like you to talk.

(*She looks at him steadily, too long for his comfort.*)

MILNE: Thanks very much for having me here. I'll go and sort myself out.

(MILNE *goes into the lighted house.* RUTH *stays in the dark.*)

'RUTH': Run. Run, you stupid bitch.

(*Night into day.*
RUTH *has gone.*
Dawn.
The jeep drives in. FRANCIS *at the wheel.* CARSON *comes out of the house, shortly followed by* GUTHRIE. GUTHRIE *has changed some of his clothes, still blue denim or something non-military. He has his camera bag and another shoulder bag.* CARSON *shouts up as though to an upstairs window.*)

CARSON: Jake! (*He turns and sees* GUTHRIE.) All set? Where's Jake?

GUTHRIE: What's that?

CARSON: Your jeep.

GUTHRIE: I can see it's a jeep. Wagner said a car.

CARSON: What's the difference? Car, jeep. This isn't a trip for a family saloon.

(GUTHRIE *is very angry and upset but still controlled.*)

GUTHRIE: A family saloon is neutral. A jeep is a target. Listen— I know the game. I know the edge on every hand I'm dealt. It was the same in the Congo, Angola, Somalia. And it's the same here.

(*Then he sees that* MILNE *has come out of the house wearing army type clothing, including a camouflage-coloured cotton bush hat.*)

(*Explodes*) Oh, *bloody hell*, he's dressed up like action man!

(GUTHRIE *takes the hat off* MILNE's *head and throws it on the ground.*)

MILNE: What's the matter?

(*He picks up the hat.*)

GUTHRIE: You don't drive into an African war in a khaki shirt with epaulettes!

CARSON: What war? There isn't going to be any war today.

MILNE: I've got a tennis shirt in my bag—I'll change if you like.

GUTHRIE: Did you bring your racket? *This is crazy.* Wagner should have done the trip.

MILNE: Thought you were on my side. Come on, Gigi—

(MILNE *goes towards the jeep, and towards* CARSON.)

62

CARSON: Got the letter?

(MILNE *pats the small bag he's carrying.*)

MILNE: Got it. (MILNE *gets into the jeep.* FRANCIS *guns the engine a little.* GUTHRIE *stands looking at the ground.*) Well, are you coming or not?

GUTHRIE: (*Quietly*) Oh, shit.

(*Then he moves quickly to the jeep, puts his camera bag on board and swings on behind as the jeep starts to move.*)

(*Blackout.*)

Act Two

The room at night.
The room occupies the whole stage now.
RUTH *sits in one of the comfortable chairs. She is wearing a long dress, not formal but loose and comfortable, perhaps a kaftan; more dressed up than we have seen her, rich material but not gaudy. She sits facing the audience.*
The room is not brightly lit, and the edges are in gloom.
MILNE *stands at the edge of the room, but is at first invisible in the darkness. He becomes visible as he begins to join in the conversation.*

'RUTH': Hello, Jacob, I'm glad it's you. I've been holding my breath since I heard the jeep. I'm glad you're back. I missed you, Jake. Actually, Jake, I . . . Christ, I've been missing you, Jake. . . .
MILNE: Hello.
RUTH: Oh—hello!
MILNE: Thought you were having a snooze.
RUTH: No, no. Good trip?
MILNE: Yes, thanks. Piece of cake.
RUTH: Lots of scoops?
MILNE: Masses.
RUTH: Come and sit down. Have a drink.
MILNE: No thanks. Where's Geoffrey?
RUTH: He's away.
MILNE: I thought everybody would be asleep.
RUTH: I felt like waiting up. Are you all right?
MILNE: Never better. (RUTH *laughs*.) What's up?

RUTH: Nothing. I like the way you have such a good time. Dashing around for the glory of the *Globe*. Grimsby man in *Globe* glory dash.

MILNE: You do think I'm naïve.

RUTH: No I don't.

MILNE: Too young and romantic.

RUTH: That's different.

MILNE: I expect I'll end up like Dick.

RUTH: I hope not.

MILNE: Dick's all right. He's a bit . . .

RUTH: Wagnerian. (*English pronunciation.*)

MILNE: I suppose he's gone off with the press corps.

RUTH: I suppose so. It's nice that you've got us to come back to.

MILNE: Yes—a line to London on tap—one couldn't ask for more. Oh—and present company included, of course.

'RUTH': Help.

MILNE: Well, I expect you'd like to go to bed.

'RUTH': I'm over here.

MILNE: I've got a piece to write.

'RUTH': To hell with that.

MILNE: You won't mind if I try to get London later?

'RUTH': And to hell with London.

MILNE: I'm sure Geoffrey wouldn't mind. Is he in KC?

'RUTH': Why don't you shut up and kiss me.

MILNE: He said I could help myself.

'RUTH': So kiss me.

MILNE: Perhaps I should try for a line first—let them know I'm here.

RUTH: I would prefer you to kiss me.

MILNE: Kiss you?

(*Pause.* RUTH *blinks and turns to him.*)

RUTH: Yes.

MILNE: Well . . . um, I was just saying, I ought to establish contact with the office.

RUTH: Yes. I think that would be a very sensible idea.

C

MILNE: Thank you.

RUTH: But isn't it rather late, or early, or something?

MILNE: It is here.

RUTH: Oh yes. We seem to have got off the subject.

MILNE: Have you been out this evening?

RUTH: No. Why?

MILNE: You look—a bit dressed up.

RUTH: This old thing? I just threw it on as I stepped out of the shower.

MILNE: Ah. Jolly nice.

RUTH: Wouldn't do for the club at all.

MILNE: Is there a club?

RUTH: The Jeddu Country Club. Very quiet since independence. They used to have Coronation dances, I believe. Now it's billiards, bar and smoking room. I don't play billiards but I drink and smoke. And they get all the important magazines—*Country Life, Mining Review, Kambawe Today* . . . and, you'll be pleased to know, some of the London papers.

MILNE: Doesn't sound bad at all. Are they flown in?

RUTH: I don't think so. We're still getting the *Morning Post*. It's all right, you don't have to kiss me at all.

MILNE: It isn't that I don't think you're attractive.

RUTH: No. It's just that Geoffrey has been damned decent to you. . . .

MILNE: Well, yes. And even if he hadn't . . .

RUTH: It wouldn't be right to make free with his possessions—his ox, his ass, his wife—

MILNE: Wait a minute. (*He pauses, concentrating for four or five seconds—he looks at her.*) No.

RUTH: Well, I'm glad it wasn't instantaneous.

MILNE: I mean your argument. It sounds good but it's not. I *might* make free with his ox and his ass—or his jeep— because they *are* merely his possessions. But if I indulged my desire for you I would be numbering you among them. As it is, it seems I regard a wife as different from a jeep,
66

which puts me in the forefront of enlightened thinking. (*Smiles*) Wouldn't you say?

RUTH: What desire for me?

MILNE: Oh, crikey.

RUTH: Had any lewd thoughts?

MILNE: I told you I found you attractive.

RUTH: Tell me about the lewd thoughts.

MILNE: No.

RUTH: Oh, come on. Don't be such a spoil-sport. There you are, in the jeep. The sun beats down. Bwana Guthrie is taking pictures of nature and poverty for the colour magazine. Tracker Francis is keeping his eye on the road. Your thoughts drift . . . 'I say, that Ruth Carson, she's all woman.' Carry on from there. (MILNE *won't*.) Did you undress me?

MILNE: No.

RUTH: I kept my clothes on?

MILNE: You undressed yourself.

RUTH: Ah. Was it dark or daylight? On a bed? On the floor? Long grass? In the jeep? (*Pause*) It was in the jeep.

MILNE: (*Sharply*) No, it wasn't. (*Pause*) It was in a parallel world. No day or night, no responsibilities, no friction, almost no gravity.

RUTH: I know it. How was I?

MILNE: (*Exasperated*) *Ruth.*

RUTH: You were *good*. It's about *time* you called me Ruth.

MILNE: Show some, then. Ruth: that which is lacking in ruthlessness. It comes into Milton. 'Look homeward angel, now, and melt with ruth.' Compassion—contrition. Something like that.

RUTH: I'm not really a tart.

MILNE: No—of course.

RUTH: I was almost a tart with my first husband, but he was a rotter in his own way. He was frankly proud of his left-hook.

MILNE: Was he?

67

RUTH: Unjustifiably so. You could slip it quite easily and get him with a right-cross. What a way to live. To get *me*, all Geoffrey had to do was clear his throat and hold the door.

MILNE: Did you love him too?

RUTH: Of course I loved him—loved Africa. Just like Deborah Kerr in *King Solomon's Mines* before the tarantula got into her petticoat. And I haven't been a tart with Geoffrey. Slipped once, but that was in a hotel room and hotel rooms shouldn't count as infidelity. They constitute a separate moral universe. Anyway, I had terrible PCR, and a tart wouldn't, would she?

MILNE: What's PCR?

RUTH: Post-coital remorse. Post-coital ruth. Quite needlessly—I mean, it's a bit metaphysical to feel guilt about the idea of Geoffrey being hurt if Geoffrey is in a blissful state of ignorance—don't you think?

MILNE: No.

RUTH: No. Fresh start. Hello!—had a good trip? (*Pause*) I don't know. I got into a state today. I'm telling you this because it is very boring, you understand. Went to bed feeling nothing more dangerous than a heightened sense of you being in the house. Woke up fluttering with imminent risk. Quite a pleasant feeling, really. Like walking along the top board knowing you don't have to jump. But a desperate feeling, too, because if you're not going to jump what the hell are you doing up there? So I got dressed to say goodbye to you. Really. Dressed for it. 'What shall I wear to say goodbye to Jake?' Don't feel flattered. You look like you look, and you've got a way of being gauche which suggests that you've got the edge on people who know the ground and prepare their effects—I was attracted, as it happens, but it's like throwing a pair when you've got three-of-a-kind on the table. This time, bingo, but no use at all to anyone looking for a straight. Anyway, while I was dressing for this intensely laconic farewell, you'd been gone an hour. Geoffrey hadn't wanted to wake me. He's thoughtful about things like

68

that. Saying goodbye would have taken care of it, I expect. It was finding you gone that did it. Quietus interruptus. I went peculiar. I lost my view of myself. I was unembarrassable. Your sheets were cold. Pillow had no smell. You say something.

MILNE: You were good, too. (*Pause*) You shouldn't try to make it sound like a free ride. 'Geoffrey will never know and I'm not his chattel so there's nothing to pay.' There are no free rides. You always pay.

RUTH: Take it, then, and pay. Be a bastard. Behave badly.

MILNE: That's better.

RUTH: Betray your benefactor.

MILNE: That's right.

RUTH: Corrupt me.

MILNE: Put it like that, I might.

RUTH: Steal me.

MILNE: I want to.

RUTH: Good. Mess up my life. I'll pay.

MILNE: Stupid.

RUTH: Don't be frightened.

MILNE: And tomorrow—

RUTH: I'll pack if you like. If you don't like, I'll stay and deadhead the bougainvillaea. Either way I'll pay.
(*They kiss on the mouth, but not passionately and not holding each other.*)

MILNE: Leave me alone. You should know better.

RUTH: I do know better. To hell with that.
(*She lets herself fall over backwards on to the sofa.* Only her calves and feet are visible.*)

MILNE: You're really something, Ruth. I don't know what.
(MILNE *turns and walks up-stage into the dark and disappears.* RUTH's *feet disappear out of sight behind the sofa and then 'she'* (*double*) *stands up with her back to the audience looking*

---

*At least that would be one way of doing this moment. In the first production she went behind the tree growing in the room, and her double came from behind the tree.

69

towards where MILNE *disappeared, undoes her dress and steps out of it (she has nothing on underneath) holding on to the dress with one hand and trailing it after her as she follows* MILNE *into the dark. Before she has disappeared* CARSON *has walked unhurriedly, relaxed, into the room from the study. He lights a cigarette and stands thoughtfully watching as* RUTH *moves into the dark. After a moment or two, behind him,* RUTH'*s voice.*)

RUTH: Got a cigarette? (*She is lying on the sofa behind* CARSON. *He turns and offers her a cigarette.* RUTH'*s hand comes into view to take it.*) Thanks. (CARSON *offers his lighter and* RUTH'*s head comes up to meet it. She stands and lights her cigarette from his lighter.*)

CARSON: There's no need for you to stay up.

RUTH: I want to.

CARSON: He may not come for hours.

RUTH: I'm all right. What time is it?

CARSON: (*Looks at his watch*) Saturday. Nearly one. You got dressed up for him.

RUTH: Well, he is the President.

(*The dog starts barking.* CARSON *moves to a light switch and the exterior lights come on. Sound of an approaching vehicle.* CARSON *leaves the room.* RUTH *moves to a chair. She puts out her cigarette. The vehicle has arrived.* CARSON'*s voice audible off-stage.*)

CARSON: (*OS*) Oh—God!

WAGNER: (*Entering*) Hello!

CARSON: (*Entering*) Any other time, old man—

WAGNER: I saw your lights from the road.

CARSON: Ruth and I were just going to bed.

WAGNER: Good evening. I brought a nightcap. (*He's carrying a bottle of Cutty Sark whisky, not a full one.*) Compliments of the firm. I'm afraid I've started without you. (*He's making himself at home. He puts the bottle down.*) I saw the lights as I was passing.

RUTH: The lights weren't on as you were passing.

CARSON: Look, Dick, not this time, there's a good fellow.

WAGNER: Have a heart—all this way for a nightcap—

CARSON: You said you were passing—

WAGNER: To see if you were up.

CARSON: Well, we were just turning in, weren't we, darling? Why don't you drop in tomorrow—*today*, for heaven's sake—for a sundowner.

RUTH: Leave off, Geoffrey—he knows. (*To* WAGNER.) You do know, don't you?

WAGNER: Oh, absolutely.

CARSON: Knows what?

RUTH: He knows we're waiting for Mageeba.

CARSON: (*Angrily*) Ruth . . .

WAGNER: Mageeba—that's the fellow.

CARSON: It's a social call. He likes to eat late.

WAGNER: Doesn't he, though?

CARSON: Well, there you are.

WAGNER: Yes, indeed. When is Colonel Shimbu supposed to be coming?

CARSON: He's not coming.

RUTH: (*Simultaneously*) In the morning. He's not coming in the morning.

CARSON: This is dreadful.

WAGNER: I'll be as quiet as a mouse.

CARSON: Mageeba is going to be furious. You'll be lucky if you don't end up under arrest.

WAGNER: I'm your house guest.

CARSON: No, you're not.

RUTH: Oh, do let him. He could crawl under the sofa. (*To* WAGNER.) You'll feel quite at home, it's almost like a bed. I'll bet you're better under a bed than in it.

CARSON: Stop this.

WAGNER: Vouch for me, then. Lobby basis, I promise.

CARSON: What do you mean, lobby basis?—this is the President of Kambawe, not some Downing Street PR man. Journalists here get hung up by their thumbs for getting his medals wrong.

WAGNER: Charming fellow, your boss.

CARSON: He's not my boss. He's the President, that's all, I can't help who's President. I'm a mining engineer.

WAGNER: They're his mines.

CARSON: They were here first and so was I. They're my bloody mines more than his.

RUTH: And more Shimbu's than yours now.

WAGNER: True.

CARSON: How did you know about all this?

WAGNER: I was guessing about Shimbu. On Mageeba I had my own source.

CARSON: Yes, I bet—Canadian loud-mouth.

WAGNER: What Canadian loud-mouth is that?

CARSON: You know about the UN team, do you?

WAGNER: Up to a point, Lord Copper.

CARSON: UN observers, they've been in KC since Sunday.

WAGNER: Shimbu's letter was to the UN not to Mageeba . . . ? Just nod your head.

CARSON: I'll brief you if you promise to leave.

WAGNER: Sounds fair.

CARSON: Mageeba wants his mines back. Last year they produced nearly sixty per cent of his copper—you read that in the *Kambawe Citizen*. The mines are no good to Shimbu because the railway goes the wrong way. You saw that on a map. So Shimbu will swop the mines for recognition of Adoma. Pretty good going—I steal your clothes and offer to give back your trousers if I can keep your shirt. He wants to talk through the UN people, the Canadians. To show good faith he says he won't fire a shot until he's fired upon.

WAGNER: Sounds sincere.

CARSON: Sounds as if he hasn't got all his armour up. Anyway, Mageeba bought it, he said he'd show up here with the Canadians at dawn, ready to talk. Half-way house, you see.

WAGNER: I'll believe the Canadians when I see them.

CARSON: Me too. Everybody's lying.

WAGNER: Tell me what you think.

CARSON: I think Shimbu wants the whole apple, and is using the time to get his supply line working. I think Mageeba isn't going to let Shimbu secede anywhere except into a ditch, and at breakfast time when he sees Shimbu hasn't fallen for it, he's going to go in with air-strikes and tanks and lose half of them in a week, and appeal to the free world about Russian interference. I also think that the British and the Americans will protest, and all the time they're protesting the Russians will be interfering the shit out of Mageeba's army, until Kambawe is about as independent as Lithuania, and that the British and Americans will protest.

WAGNER: I see. I'll make sure the *Globe* puts that over.

CARSON: You'll what—?

WAGNER: I said I'll make sure the *Globe*—

(*But* CARSON *is already laughing heartily.*)

CARSON: Oh good! Oh wonderful! The *Globe* will pronounce! We're saved—the Prime Minister will be straight on to the Foreign Office— (*He mimes winding up an old-fashioned telephone while holding the ear-piece.*) 'Now look here, have you seen what those Russkies are up to in Africa?—the Queen is absolutely *furious* and so is Albert!'

WAGNER: All right.

RUTH: Poor Dick.

CARSON: Well . . . there you are.

WAGNER: Thanks, Geoff.

(WAGNER *helps himself to a drink.*)

CARSON: You said you'd leave.

WAGNER: I was lying.

CARSON: I'm beginning to wonder if you can be altogether trusted.

WAGNER: I'm sorry, but nobody on this story has got a sight of Mageeba since it broke. Let alone a quote. Let alone an interview. Let alone this Shimbu deal. It's too big to pass up and I'm greedy for it—I admit that. I'm going to put the *Globe* so far out in front this Sunday, those roving correspondents and African specialists and line-shooters and

73

bullshitters won't keep down their dinner for a week.

CARSON: Serve you right if he doesn't show up. He seldom does what he says.

(*But a car is becoming audible.*)

WAGNER: If he hadn't shown up I'd still be watching the compound. I saw him land fifteen minutes ago. Also two Sea King helicopters. Do you think they're full of Canadian lawyers?

(*The car is getting louder.*)

CARSON: Are you going?

WAGNER: No.

CARSON: Be careful if he laughs.

(CARSON *goes out to meet the car.*)

RUTH: You're shaking.

WAGNER: That's because I'm scared. What do I call him?

RUTH: He likes to be called boy.

WAGNER: For Christ's sake.

RUTH: I'm beginning to like you a little.

WAGNER: Don't leave the room.

(*Then* MAGEEBA *is in, followed by* CARSON. MAGEEBA *is in uniform, open-necked shirt, informal but well-laundered and wearing medal-ribbon. He carries a short cane with a metal knob. He is holding a convincing machine-gun, with which he fires a burst. It is a toy.*)

MAGEEBA: Mrs Carson . . . a little present for your son. . . . (*He gives the gun to* RUTH.)

RUTH: Good evening, Your Excellency . . . how kind of you to honour us.

MAGEEBA: A pleasure . . . a beautiful home and a beautiful hostess. Please forgive this late hour.

RUTH: It's never too late—welcome . . . we're night birds here.

MAGEEBA: How gracious . . . I, too, sleep very little.

RUTH: (*Gaily*) Well—uneasy lies the head that—

'RUTH': (*Loudly*) Idiot!

(*She has reflexively fired a burst from the gun.*)

74

RUTH: I mean the sheer volume of work must be enormous, the cares of State, and—

'RUTH': Shut up, you silly woman—

RUTH: May I introduce Mr Richard Wagner?

MAGEEBA: Mr Wagner.

WAGNER: Sir—your most—er—Excellency—

'RUTH': Compose yourself, Wagner.

MAGEEBA: You are a visitor to Kambawe?

WAGNER: Yes, sir.

CARSON: Would you care for anything, sir?

MAGEEBA: What brings you to Kambawe?

WAGNER: You do, sir—your determined stand against Russian imperialism in Africa has won the admiration of the British people, sir—

'RUTH': Jesus Christ.

WAGNER: And I feel very privileged myself to have the opportunity to—

(MAGEEBA stops him with an upraised hand.)

MAGEEBA: (Triumphantly) Ah! (To CARSON.) Your guest is a journalist.

CARSON: I'm very sorry about this, sir—Mr Wagner arrived a few minutes ago quite by chance—he was just leaving—

RUTH: For London.

MAGEEBA: How I envy him. I have very happy memories of London. Student days, you know. I learned everything about economic theory. It has proved a great handicap. (To RUTH.) How are things in London, Mrs Carson?

RUTH: Oh—did you know I'd been?

MAGEEBA: My cousin tells me of all interesting and distinguished travellers.

RUTH: You have a cousin at the airport?

MAGEEBA: No, at the Court of St James.

'RUTH': Say goodnight, Gracie.

MAGEEBA: But I also have a cousin at the airport, of course.

RUTH: Oh good.

MAGEEBA: You see, Mrs Carson, I am like a father to all citizens

75

of Kambawe. In your case, of course, that is difficult to imagine.

RUTH: Of course.

'RUTH': Wrong!

MAGEEBA: Such is our legacy of racial and cultural prejudice.

RUTH: Yes, indeed.

'RUTH': (*Loudly*) Geoffrey!!

(WAGNER *decides to make his pitch and to do so quite formally. The effect is more wooden than formal.*)

WAGNER: Your Excellency—Sir . . . I hope you will forgive my presence but as I say, the British people are watching with intense and sympathetic interest your courageous stand against the communist menace in Africa, and if you, sir, have any words of reassurance—however few—any message for the British people—and indeed the world—the *Sunday Globe* would be privileged to publish them.

(*Pause.* MAGEEBA *has been deciding on a chair and sinking himself into it. Now he looks up and looks at* WAGNER *apologetically.*)

MAGEEBA: I'm so sorry—Mr Wagner—were you speaking to me?

WAGNER: (*Gamely*) Yes, sir. I was saying, Your Excellency, that the British people are following with intense admiration and interest your . . . er . . . courageous stand against the communist threat in Africa . . . sir . . .

MAGEEBA: Yes?

WAGNER: Yes, sir, and if you have any message for the British people—and indeed the world—well, my paper would be privileged to publish it.

MAGEEBA: (*Pause*) The *Sunday Globe*.

(WAGNER *nods.*)

'RUTH': Run.

CARSON: Well, Dick, it's time you were off.

MAGEEBA: Is Mr Wagner a friend of yours, Geoffrey?

CARSON: No—

RUTH: (*Simultaneously*) Oh, rather. We met in London. I'm

76

terribly fond of him. (*To* WAGNER.) I'll see you to the door.
(*Pause. Finally,* WAGNER *moves to leave.*)

MAGEEBA: Do you have to leave, Mr Wagner?

WAGNER: Not at all.

MAGEEBA: Then you must stay. I am interested to meet you. We must have a good talk. Sit down there.

WAGNER: Thank you, sir.

'RUTH': You're bitched, Wagner.

CARSON: (*Worriedly*) Your Excellency . . .

MAGEEBA: Yes, you were saying, Geoffrey—a little whisky and water, then.

CARSON: Of course. Would you like the malt?

MAGEEBA: Not with water.

CARSON: No—of course.

MAGEEBA: The blended, about half and half, no ice.

CARSON: Whisky and water, no ice.

WAGNER: That will do me nicely, without the water. (WAGNER *is transformed, secure, pleased with himself.*) So I don't mind a bit of malt if you can spare it.
(CARSON *uses* WAGNER's *bottle of Cutty Sark for the drinks.*)

CARSON: (*To* RUTH) Darling?

RUTH: Nothing.

CARSON: Ruth has arranged for a little late supper to be laid out in the dining room if you should care for something, sir.

'RUTH': He's not going to have room for a thing after Wagner.

MAGEEBA: Mr . . . Wagner.

WAGNER: Mr . . . President. Sir.

MAGEEBA: Mr Wagner, it is not you, is it, who has to be congratulated on the *Sunday Globe*'s interview with Colonel Shimbu?

WAGNER: That wasn't me, sir, no. As a matter of fact, it wasn't a *Globe* reporter at all, it was a young freelance chap who found himself caught up with Shimbu quite by accident. Of course when he sent it to the *Globe*, they were bound to use it, because—well, all the news that's fit to print, as they say.

77

MAGEEBA: 'The press lives by disclosure.'

WAGNER: Ah, you know that one.

MAGEEBA: Delane of *The Times*—we had all that at the LSE. The political history of communications, or some such course. (*He accepts his drink from* CARSON.) Thank you. And C. P. Scott of the *Manchester Guardian*, of course— 'Comment is free but facts are sacred.'

WAGNER: Yes, and 'Comment is free but facts are on expenses.'

MAGEEBA: Scott?

WAGNER: Wagner. (*He takes his drink.*) Cheers.

MAGEEBA: What did you think of the Shimbu interview by the way?

WAGNER: Ah well (*He looks for safe ground.*)—these chaps, they even talk like puppets, don't they? I think it's useful in a way to let them have their say. For that reason. Of course, sir, if you felt that some reply—or refutation—was indicated, I need hardly say that I, or rather the *Globe*—

MAGEEBA: You would give me equal space?

WAGNER: Oh—absolutely—

MAGEEBA: That's very fair. Isn't it Geoffrey? Mr Wagner says I can have equal space.

WAGNER: And some space is more equal than others. I think, sir, I could more or less guarantee that an interview with you at this juncture of the war would be treated as the main news story of the day, and of course would be picked up by newspapers, and all the media, round the world.

MAGEEBA: What war, Mr Wagner?

WAGNER: Sorry?

MAGEEBA: Kambawe is not at war. We have a devolution problem. I believe you have one, too.

WAGNER: A devolution problem? Yes . . . I see. Do you mind, sir, if I make a note or two?

(MAGEEBA *waves permission and* WAGNER *takes a notebook from his pocket.*)

MAGEEBA: If it is a war it is not of my waging. I am a man of peace . . . (*He waits for* WAGNER *and repeats as he writes.*)

man of peace. When a man strikes me without cause or warning, I invite him to breakfast. Don't I, Geoffrey?

CARSON: I have told Mr Wagner that this is a social call, sir.

MAGEEBA: Quite right. I am going to have breakfast with Shimbu. At least—I have invited him to breakfast, I can do no more than that, and I don't mind at all, Mr Wagner, that you are here to witness my good faith.

WAGNER: Absolutely.

'RUTH': Absolutely. Help.

(RUTH *moves apart and is lost in her thoughts.*)

WAGNER: Do you think Shimbu will come?

MAGEEBA: Yes. He might come early perhaps and bring his own food but I think he will come. It would be to his advantage now to come to the table with a reasonable and peace-loving man. His methods have been piratical but his cause is not without interest. Our frontiers, you know, are still the frontiers of colonialism. Adoma has its own language, an ancient culture and the people are of distinct appearance. This does not mean that Adoma could prosper as an independent nation. Frankly it could not, except as the hand maiden of its so-called liberators, and I think Shimbu will see that there is more true independence in being—let us say—an autonomous state federated to Kambawe.

WAGNER: Are you offering that, sir?

MAGEEBA: I would consider a referendum. But of course that would depend on an immediate withdrawal from his present aggressive positions.

WAGNER: The Malakuangazi mines.

MAGEEBA: I don't think Geoffrey would accept anything less?

CARSON: He did rather come in without knocking.

MAGEEBA: And of course there is the question of uninvited foreigners. At this moment on Kambawe soil we have Russians, Cubans, Yemeni and Libyans. We even have a few Czech and German mechanics, I'm told. The American Ambassador asked me if I would let the United Nations come in. I said, half of them are already here—working for Shimbu.

WAGNER: Is there any UN presence in Kamba City yet?

MAGEEBA: No.

WAGNER: I see. And what if Shimbu doesn't come to the table and doesn't withdraw?

MAGEEBA: Then, Mr Wagner, you may call it a war.

WAGNER: When may I do that, sir?

MAGEEBA: Would ten a.m. suit you?

(WAGNER *grins, drains his glass and holds it out to* CARSON.)

WAGNER: (*To* CARSON) May I . . . ?

'RUTH': On a packet of salt used in my grandmother's kitchen there was a label showing a girl holding a packet of salt with the label showing, and so on. It is said, with what authority I do not know, that this was the inspiration of Whistler's famous painting of my grandmother painting her self-portrait, the one he was painting. A different school holds that it was in fact the inspiration of Turner's painting of a packet of salt. During a storm at sea. Sorry. I was miles away. Come and sit down. I talk to myself in the middle of a conversation. In fact I talk to myself in the middle of an *imaginary* conversation, which is itself a refuge from some other conversation altogether, frequently imaginary. I hope you don't mind me telling you all this.

WAGNER: Do you have what you need to win the war?

MAGEEBA: If it's a short war.

WAGNER: And if it's not? Are you looking to us and the Americans?

MAGEEBA: I'd be a fool to do that. Your record of cowardice in Africa stretches from Angola to Eritrea.

CARSON: Lobby basis, Dick.

MAGEEBA: No—no—I don't believe in that. They asked me if they could appoint a lobby correspondent in KC. I said, fine, tell him to go and sit in the Sheraton, it's the most comfortable lobby in town. I know the British press is very attached to the lobby system. It lets the journalists and the politicians feel proud of their traditional freedoms while giving the reader as much of the truth as they think is good for him. I have some experience of the British press. When you granted us our independence—as Geoffrey likes to refer to the military victory of the Nationalist Front—the Kambawe paper was the property of an English gentleman. Isn't that so, Geoffrey?

CARSON: Well, not exactly, sir—

MAGEEBA: Not exactly a gentleman, no, but a rich Englishman with a title. So there we were, an independent country, and the only English newspaper was still part of a British Empire—a family empire—a chain of newspapers—a fleet of newspapers, shall I say? Yes, that's very good, not a chain but a fleet of newspapers. That's good, isn't it, Mr Wagner?

WAGNER: Yes . . . you mean like a convoy?

'RUTH': He means like Fleet Street, you fool.

MAGEEBA: Fleet Street—

WAGNER: Oh yes—very good—

MAGEEBA: Of course, we had many businesses controlled by overseas interests, we still have many, and we have many more partnerships—even the Kambawe Mining Corporation is such a partnership and you can see from that, can you not, Mr Wagner, that we have no prejudice against English gentlemen as such—but a newspaper, a newspaper is not like a mine, or a bank, or an airline; it is the voice of the people and the Kambawe paper was the voice of an English millionaire.

WAGNER: Which one?

CARSON: Yours, Dick.

WAGNER: Oh . . . somewhat before my time, sir.

MAGEEBA: Nothing personal, Mr Wagner.

WAGNER: Good God, I hold no brief for *him*.

MAGEEBA: I realize of course that you are only an able-seaman on the flag-ship.

WAGNER: Well, sir, we've come a long way since we were galley slaves. Northcliffe could sack a man for wearing the wrong

81

hat. Literally. There was a thing called the *Daily Mail* hat, and he expected his reporters to wear it. Things are very different now.

MAGEEBA: Indeed, Mr Wagner, now the hat your proprietor expects you to wear is metaphorical only.

WAGNER: With respect, sir, you underestimate the strength of the organized workers—the journalists—I'm with you on this one, if I may say so, sir—a newspaper is too important to be merely a rich man's property.

MAGEEBA: Yes. There is nothing to be said for private ownership. The power of the proprietor is too limited to do any good.

WAGNER: Too limited?

MAGEEBA: Naturally.A proprietor can only dismiss you from his *own* newspaper. The irresponsible journalist remains free to work elsewhere. No, I'm with you on this one, if I may say so, Mr Wagner. Collective responsibility. Let the journalists close ranks and be answerable to no one but themselves.

(WAGNER *suspects he is being out-flanked.*)

WAGNER: Yes . . . well, they would be answerable to a democratically elected body representing the membership.

MAGEEBA: That's what I said. What do you think, Mrs Carson?

(RUTH *hasn't been listening but she is equal to the occasion.*)

RUTH: I think I'll have that drink after all.

(*She goes to get it.*)

MAGEEBA: (*To* RUTH) Yes, we should drink to Mr Wagner's freedom.

RUTH: Is it in question?

(*She is momentarily concerned, but* CARSON *explains.*)

CARSON: His freedom to report.

RUTH: Ah, yes.

MAGEEBA: (*Raising his glass*) To the downfall of the English millionaires.

CARSON: I'm not sure that I ought to drink to that. I think I'm related to one or two.

MAGEEBA: Do they have newspapers?

CARSON: Oh, no, they're entirely respectable. (*To* WAGNER.) Well, Dick, to freedom from millionaires—

RUTH: How strange. I had no idea that it was the millionaires who were threatening your freedom to report, Dick. *I* thought it was a millionaire who was picking up the *bill* for your freedom to report. In fact, I was discussing this very thing with somebody only yesterday—who could it have been?—oh, yes, it was Alastair. . . . (*She smiles broadly at* WAGNER.)

WAGNER: (*Sarcastically*) Alastair, was it?

RUTH: 'Allie,' I said, 'how *are* things in London with all those millionaires controlling the freedom to report?' 'I don't think I quite follow you, Mummy,' he said. 'The whole country is littered with papers pushing every political line from anarchy to Zen.' *His* theory—Alastair's theory—is that it's the very free-for-all which guarantees the freedom of each. 'You see, Mummy,' he said, 'you don't have to be a millionaire to contradict one. It isn't the millionaires who are going to stop you, it's the Wagners who don't trust the public to choose the marked card.' Do you think he's got something, Dick?

WAGNER: I was talking about *national* papers.

RUTH: (*Eagerly*) That's *just* what I said to him. 'Allie,' I said, as I spread his Marmite, 'it's absurd to equate the freedom of the millionaires to push *their* line with the freedom of a basement pamphleteer to challenge them.' 'Oh, Mummy,' he said, 'don't be so *silly*. You are confusing freedom with capability. The *Flat Earth News* is *free* to sell a million copies. What it lacks is the *capability* of finding a million people with four pence and a conviction that the earth is flat. You see, Mummy,' he said, 'people don't buy rich men's papers because the men are rich: the men are rich because people buy their papers.' Honestly, the things they

83

teach them at Ascot Heath!

WAGNER: You pointed out, did you, that a man can be rich from oil or real estate and subsidize a paper on the profits?

RUTH: Of course. But he was ready for that one—apparently some of the chaps were thrashing it out in the boot-room after footer, and the general concensus of opinion among the Lower Third is that freedom is neutral. Free expression includes a state of affairs where *any* millionaire can have a national newspaper, if that's what it costs. A state of affairs, Allie says, where only a particular approved, licensed, and supervised non-millionaire can have a newspaper is called, for example, Russia.

MAGEEBA: Or, of course, Kambawe.

'RUTH': Geoffrey!

CARSON: I'm sorry, sir—I know Ruth didn't mean—

MAGEEBA: (*Placatingly*) Please!

RUTH: I *am* sorry—he's such a chatterbox, Allie . . .

MAGEEBA: Please don't concern yourself. I enjoy a free and open debate. It is a luxury which a man in my position can seldom afford. And I admit that by the highest ideals the *Daily Citizen* is open to criticism. But you must remember it is the only English language paper we have. The population cannot yet support a number of competing papers offering a natural balance of opinion.

CARSON: Exactly.

MAGEEBA: At the time of independence the *Daily Citizen* was undoubtedly free. It was free to select the news it thought fit to print, to make much of it, or little, and free to make room for more and more girls wearing less and less underwear. You may smile, but does freedom of the press mean freedom to choose its own standards?

CARSON: Absolutely.

MAGEEBA: Mrs Carson?

RUTH: What's the alternative?

MAGEEBA: That was the question. Easy enough to shut the paper down, as I would have been obliged to do had it not been

84

burned down during the state of emergency which followed independence. But what to put in its place? The English millionaire folded his singed tents and stole away the insurance money, which didn't belong to him since I had nationalized the paper well before the fire was out. Never mind—the field was open. I did not believe a newspaper should be part of the apparatus of the state; we are not a totalitarian society. But neither could I afford a return to the whims of private enterprise. I had the immense and delicate task of restoring confidence in Kambawe. I could afford the naked women but not the naked scepticism, the carping and sniping and the public washing of dirty linen which represents freedom to an English editor. What then? A democratic committee of journalists?—a thorn bush for the editor to hide in. No, no—freedom with responsibility, that was the elusive formula we pondered all those years ago at the LSE. And that is what I found. From the ashes there arose, by public subscription, a new *Daily Citizen*, responsible and relatively free. (*He leans towards* WAGNER.) Do you know what I mean by a relatively free press, Mr Wagner?

WAGNER: Not exactly, sir, no.

MAGEEBA: I mean a free press which is edited by one of my relatives.

(*He throws back his head and laughs.* WAGNER *joins in uncertainly.* RUTH *smiles nervously.* CARSON *looks scared.* MAGEEBA *brings the weighted end of his stick down on* WAGNER'*s head.*)

(*Shouting*) So it doesn't go crawling to uppity niggers!—so it doesn't let traitors shit on the front page!—so it doesn't go sucking up to liars and criminals! 'Yes sir, Colonel Shimbu, tell us about the exploitation of your people!— free speech for all here, Colonel Shimbu, tell us about the wonderful world you're going to build in that vulture's garbage dump you want to call a country'—yes, you tell us before you get a machine-gun up your backside and your brains coming down your nostrils!—who's going to interview you *then*, Colonel, sir!

(MAGEEBA *has stood up and moved away from* WAGNER.
WAGNER's *head is bleeding slightly above the hairline.*)

(*Evenly*) I'll give him equal space. Six foot long and six foot
deep, just like any other traitor and communist jackal.

(*A vehicle—a jeep—draws up outside.*)

CARSON: (*Alert*) Shimbu?

(MAGEEBA *draws himself up.* CARSON *goes to the door but before
he gets there* GUTHRIE *enters. He is somewhat the worse for
wear. He glances round the room and then ignores everybody
and walks diagonally right down-stage to where* WAGNER *is.
His words are only for* WAGNER.)

GUTHRIE: Dick. Jacob's dead.

CARSON: (*In response to* MAGEEBA's *glance of enquiry*) This is
Mr Guthrie, Your Excellency, he is also from—er—London—

(GUTHRIE *crosses to* MAGEEBA *and stands close to him.*)

GUTHRIE: Are you the President of this shit-house country?

WAGNER: George . . .

GUTHRIE: Is it you runs that drunken duck-shoot calls itself an
army?

(WAGNER *and* CARSON *are moving in on him.* WAGNER *grabs*
GUTHRIE *and starts pulling him away.*)

(*Shouts*) I don't call that a fucking cease-fire! I hope they
blow their fucking heads off!

(WAGNER *has got* GUTHRIE *back down into a chair, and holds
him down.* RUTH *comes forward.*)

RUTH: Where's Jacob?

GUTHRIE: In the jeep.

RUTH: In the jeep? What's he doing there?

(GUTHRIE *says nothing.* RUTH *starts to leave.*)

GUTHRIE: (*Sharply*) Don't turn him over—he'll come away in
your hand.

(RUTH *moans and sinks down where she is.*)

WAGNER: Jesus.

CARSON: I'm sorry. What happened?

GUTHRIE: We never got to Shimbu.

MAGEEBA: Your messenger, Geoffrey?

CARSON: Yes. (*To* GUTHRIE.) Have you got the letter?

GUTHRIE: Jake had it. I suppose it's still in his bag.

(CARSON *leaves the room.*)

(*To* WAGNER) You've got blood on your head.

MAGEEBA: Well, Mrs Carson. I must say goodnight. Thank you for your gracious hospitality. (*To* WAGNER.) I will remember what you said, Mr Wagner.

WAGNER: What was that . . . sir?

MAGEEBA: Why, that my determined stand against communist imperialism is being watched with admiration by the British people.

WAGNER: Oh, yes.

MAGEEBA: Congratulations on your Mageeba interview. Oh—did you have any further questions?

WAGNER: No, I don't think so.

MAGEEBA: I shall look forward to reading the *Sunday Globe* this week. The main news story of the day, I think you said. I take my hat off to you. I'm sorry if I was rude about yours. Oh, one more thing, Mr Wagner—would you make a note. . . . It was not Othello I played at Charterhouse. It was Caliban. They always get it wrong.

(MAGEEBA *leaves.*)

GUTHRIE: He hit you? Because he didn't like your hat?

WAGNER: That's right. What happened to Jacob?

GUTHRIE: It was right outside Malakuangazi. Just getting dark. It took us twice as long to get there as Geoffrey said. Mageeba's pass worked but it worked slowly. Everybody scared stiff of getting their ears chopped off for letting us through, and also for *not* letting us through. Same thing round here, I mean the road to the house. There's soldiers behind every tree. A real back-up to the peace initiative.

WAGNER: Yeah, he was going to have Shimbu for breakfast all right.

GUTHRIE: These are the good guys. We get accredited by the good guys.

RUTH: I want to know what happened.

> (MAGEEBA's *car has been heard to leave.* CARSON *enters with a first-aid box. He attends briefly to* WAGNER's *wound while* GUTHRIE *talks.*)

GUTHRIE: We eventually got to the front, which is where the cover runs out. You could see Malakuangazi across a strip of open land, no dead ground. We had the headlights on, acting friendly, and a white handkerchief tied to the aerial, but it was just about dark, they couldn't see what was coming. We got a couple of hundred yards, and they put up a flare. That was okay. But somebody behind us got nervous and let off a few rounds. You know—shooting at a town with a rifle—that sort of discipline. So that gets somebody else excited, and pretty soon there's a cross-fire, and another flare, and we're the only moving object in sight. There's only one smart thing to do and the driver knows it. He stops the jeep and runs and I shouted to Jake to run and I got fifty yards and when I looked back he's in the driving seat trying to turn the jeep round. He got it round, and then he was hit. Knocked him into the back seat. I should have looked after him better. Stupid sod. Up 'til then he was having a good time.

WAGNER: You went back to the jeep.

GUTHRIE: I didn't know if he was dead. Engine was okay. Only the windscreen smashed. So I killed the lights and drove it back. But he was dead all right. A whole burst, head and shoulders. Heavy machine-gun, I should think, just spraying around. He didn't know anything about it anyway.

CARSON: Where's Francis?

GUTHRIE: He ran the other way, towards Shimbu.

CARSON: Why?

GUTHRIE: I don't know. Maybe he knew something.

CARSON: My God. You were taking a hell of a chance, going in after dark.

GUTHRIE: We were already six hours behind.

CARSON: Shimbu was a long shot anyway.

GUTHRIE: Not Shimbu. The *Globe* is a Sunday paper. If you miss it by an hour you've missed it by a week. Story could be dead as a—I mean—(*To* WAGNER.) he wanted to go in, Dick. It wasn't just me.

(WAGNER *nods.* CARSON *touches* RUTH's *shoulder.*)

CARSON: I've got to follow Mageeba to KC. There's nothing to worry about. He needs to talk to me about the mines, doesn't want to bomb the bits that matter. (*To* WAGNER.) I'm taking the helicopter. I'll dump you two at the airport, but after that you're on your own. Get on any plane you can, and with luck you'll be out of the country before Mageeba has time to think about you. He's got bigger problems at the moment.

WAGNER: I want to file from here.

CARSON: I'm already sticking my neck out for you. You've got time to get out and file.

WAGNER: No, I don't like that—planes can be late. Let me think.

GUTHRIE: You can file first from KC. Get an AP wire. You have to risk that. And then a plane. Gives you two chances.

WAGNER: Yes, that's good. Okay. What about Jake?

CARSON: There's no proper morgue in Jeddu. I'll take the body to KC. Do you know anything about his family? Who to tell?

WAGNER: Only the *Globe.* I'd better let them know that at least. All right?

CARSON: You can try.

(WAGNER *goes to the telex and switches it on, and taps some keys.*)

We'll take the jeep down to the compound.

WAGNER: (*Over his shoulder to* GUTHRIE) Jeep picture?

(GUTHRIE *pats his camera bag.*)

GUTHRIE: I shot a couple of rolls before starting back. It was an artillery war when I left.

CARSON: (*To* WAGNER) If you can't get straight through you'll have to leave it.

WAGNER: All my stuff's at the hotel.

89

CARSON: Forget it.

WAGNER: And the car?

CARSON: I'll get it picked up some time.

GUTHRIE: It's my car. I want it.

(WAGNER *leaves the telex and comes back to* GUTHRIE.)

WAGNER: What do you mean? Are you going back to
Malakuangazi?

GUTHRIE: I thought I would, yes.

WAGNER: There's always other stories, Gigi.

GUTHRIE: I fancy this one.

(GUTHRIE *is putting rolls of exposed film into linen envelopes
which are pre-prepared, labelled.*)

Here. The guy in the AP office is called Chamberlain.
Ask him to print up this one—I marked it—and wire
anything which looks worthwhile. Tell him to push it to
eight hundred and bugger the grain, I was using moonlight
and flares. This one is for the London plane if you can get
a pigeon.

CARSON: I don't think you understand. Mageeba is unpredictable.
He may decide he was amused by your effrontery and give
you a decoration, or he may feed you to the crocodiles. If I
were you I wouldn't take the chance. He can always post
you the decoration.

GUTHRIE: No, I don't think so.

CARSON: *Look*—first that Shimbu interview, and now you calling
him names—he's not going to think the *Globe* is on his side.

GUTHRIE: We're not here to be on somebody's side, Geoffrey.
That was World World II. We try to show what happened,
and what it was like. That's all we do, and sometimes
people bitch about which side we're supposed to be on. (*To*
WAGNER.) Remember that brasshat in Saigon? 'When are
you going to get on the team?' Remember that? The team.
Give me the keys. I'll go by the hotel and get your stuff out.

(WAGNER *hands over the car keys.*)

WAGNER: Use my room. You should crash for a few hours.

GUTHRIE: No, I want to get back. It'll all be happening this

90

morning.

WAGNER: I'll see you then. Take care, George.

CARSON: Good luck, George.

RUTH: I hope they blow your head off, George.

CARSON: Come on, Ruth.

RUTH: No, I won't. (*To* GUTHRIE.) Tell me something, George. Which page is it on?

GUTHRIE: What?

(*The newspapers are still in the room and* RUTH *picks up one of them.*)

RUTH: This thing that's worth dying for.

GUTHRIE: I don't intend to die for anything.

RUTH: Jake did.

GUTHRIE: Yes.

RUTH: (*With the paper*) Show me where it is. It can't be on the back page—'Rain Halts Australian Collapse.' That's not it, is it? Or the woman's page—'Sexy Or Sexist?—The Case For Intimate Deodorants.' Is that it, George? What about readers' letters?—'Dear Sir, If the Prime Minister had to travel on the seven fifty-three from Bexhill every morning we'd soon have the railwaymen back on the lines.' Am I getting warm, George?

WAGNER: You're belittling his death.

RUTH: (*Angrily*) You bet I am. I'm not going to let you think he died for free speech and the guttering candle of democracy —crap! You're all doing it to impress each other and be top dog the next time you're propping up a bar in Beirut or Bangkok, or Chancery Lane. Look at Dick and tell me I'm a liar. He's going to be a hero. The wires from London are going to burn up with congratulations. They'll be talking about Wagner's scoop for years, or anyway Wagner will. It's all bloody ego. And the winner isn't democracy, it's just business. As far as I'm concerned, Jake died for the product. He died for the women's page, and the crossword, and the racing results, and the heartbreak beauty queens and somewhere at the end of a long list I suppose he died for the

91

leading article too, but it's never worth *that*—
(*She has started to swipe at* GUTHRIE *with a newspaper and she ends up flinging it at him. She moves away.* GUTHRIE *moves to go.*)

GUTHRIE: (*To* WAGNER) What's the name of the hotel?

WAGNER: I forget. Green awnings.

CARSON: The Sandringham.

WAGNER: Oh yeah. I should have used that.
(GUTHRIE *goes over to* RUTH.)

GUTHRIE: I've been around a lot of places. People do awful things to each other. But it's worse in places where everybody is kept in the dark. It really is. Information is light. Information, in itself, about anything, is light. That's all you can say, really.
(GUTHRIE *goes.*)

CARSON: Go to bed, darling. I'm sorry about having to go. I'll bring Allie back anyway.

RUTH: Will it be all right for him here?

CARSON: Oh yes. If it's not, I don't want you here either. I'll have some news before I leave KC. (*To* WAGNER.) Fit?
(*The telex has started chattering.*)
If that's London make it quick. (*To* RUTH.) Do we have an old blanket or something like that?

RUTH: Just take anything.
(CARSON *goes out.* WAGNER *has gone to the chattering telex. It doesn't chatter for long.* WAGNER *stands reading the message as it comes off the machine. The machine stops.* WAGNER *continues to stare at it for a few moments. Then he turns away and goes to his Cutty Sark bottle and pours himself a drink and then takes the drink back to his chair and sits down.*)
London?

WAGNER: Yes.

RUTH: Well?

WAGNER: There's no hurry.
(CARSON *comes back with a ground-sheet.*)

CARSON: Allie's ground-sheet. I'll get him another one. (*To*

WAGNER.) Okay—? What are you doing? (*He's crossing to the telex.*) Did you get it? (CARSON *tears the message out of the machine and looks at it. He comes back into the room with it.*) It's yours. From someone called Battersby. 'Milne copy blacked by subs, full chapel and machine room support. Total confrontation and dismissal notices tonight, weekend shut down definite. Wotwu—'—is that a garble?—'Wotwu —Battersby.' What's that?

WAGNER: There's no paper this week.

CARSON: What about your story?

(*Pause*)

That's rotten luck, Dick.

(*He gives* WAGNER *the telex message.*)

WAGNER: Yeah. Wotwu.

CARSON: What is that?

WAGNER: Workers of the world unite.

CARSON: I see. What will you do now?

WAGNER: I'm just thinking. Would you air-freight George's film for me? There's no rush.

(CARSON *receives the envelopes from* WAGNER, *or just picks them up.*)

CARSON: Yes, all right.

WAGNER: Telex the way-bill number to the office and they'll pick them up COD. I'll call the hotel and get George to come back and fetch me. There may be a paper next week, and as he says, it'll all be happening this morning. I ought to be there.

RUTH: Aren't you supposed to be withdrawing your labour?

WAGNER: (*Snaps at her*) Don't get clever with me, damn you.

(*Pause. To* CARSON.) I'm sorry.

RUTH: That's all right.

CARSON: What about your story? Can't they do anything with it?

WAGNER: Yes, they could make paper aeroplanes with it. We'll see. Thanks for everything, Geoff.

CARSON: Drop by again.

WAGNER: I will.

CARSON: (*To* RUTH) I'll phone from KC.

(CARSON *leaves.* WAGNER *empties his glass and stands up.*)

WAGNER: Could I have another drink?

RUTH: You brought it. (*She takes his glass.*) I think I'll have one too. Nightcap.

(WAGNER *goes to the telex and is tapping at it while she is pouring the rest of the Cutty Sark equally into two glasses.*) What are you doing?

WAGNER: Short piece about Jake. Onpass *Grimsby Messenger.*

RUTH: Good idea.

(*The jeep is heard leaving.*)

No point in staying sober now he's gone, eh?

WAGNER: Jake?

RUTH: The President.

WAGNER: Oh.

(*She takes his drink and puts it on top of the telex.*)

RUTH: Are you going to call George?

WAGNER: In a while. He won't be there yet. Did you have a thing for Jake?

RUTH: No.

WAGNER: Just wondered.

(WAGNER *is working the keyboard, pausing for thought. He stops to loosen his tie and light a cigarette.* RUTH *takes her drink back into the room.*)

RUTH: Well, it was a very elevated, intellectual sort of thing. I wanted to undress him with my teeth. Oh God, I'm tired as hell and I'm not going to get to sleep.

WAGNER: Don't you have a pill for that?

RUTH: There *are* no pills for that. I want to be hammered out, disjointed, folded up and put away like linen in a drawer. (*She goes back to the whisky bottle and holds it upside down over her glass, and examines the label.*) You can use the phone upstairs if you like.

WAGNER: I thought you didn't want to be a tart. . . .

RUTH: How do I know until I've tried it? I name this bottle 'Cutty Sark'.

(*She breaks the bottle against the marble shelf and drops the*

remainder into the bin. She looks at WAGNER: *he's at the
keyboard, tie loose, cigarette in mouth, whisky on the 'piano
lid'. It looks like a familiar piano-player-plus-singer scene. We
hear the piano. 'The Lady is a Tramp'.*)

'RUTH': (*Sings*) She gets too hungry for dinner at eight,
                Loves the theatre but never comes late,
                She doesn't bother with people she hates,
                That's why the lady—
(WAGNER *disrupts this by tearing the paper out of the machine.
He leaves the telex and stands next to* RUTH.)

RUTH: Is that it?

WAGNER: That's it.
    (*Blackout.*)